TIM MOSS

CLOSE TO THE EDGE

A COLLECTION OF IMAGINATIVE SHORT STORIES WITH A TWIST IN THE TALE

TIM MOSS

CLOSE TO THE EDGE

A COLLECTION OF IMAGINATIVE SHORT STORIES WITH A TWIST IN THE TALE

MEREO
Cirencester

Published by Mereo

Mereo is an imprint of Memoirs Publishing

25 Market Place, Cirencester, Gloucestershire, GL7 2NX
info@memoirsbooks.co.uk   www.memoirspublishing.com

CLOSE TO THE EDGE

ISBN: 978-1-909544-56-7

AUTHOR PROFILE

Tim Moss was born in Bedford, United Kingdom in 1954. He studied medicine at Bristol University and has worked as a neuroscientist and a pathologist. He has published numerous articles in medical and scientific journals and authored several professional reference books. This is his first work of fiction.

CONTENTS

THE MONKEY EATER

"It is certainly most extraordinary. May I ask how you came by it?"

Jules turned the object over to inspect its base, then looked back up at the dealer's face. He had a dark complexion; more Indian blood than Spanish, he decided. The row of mummified human heads under glass domes on the shelf behind him lent a rather macabre atmosphere to the proceedings.

"My associate Diego Gonzales is based in Martinique" the dealer replied. "He bought it from an Arawak native in the street market in El Callao. Apparently the Indian found it near Angel Falls in the Guiana highlands." He smiled, revealing several gold teeth. "I can assure you it is genuine."

Jules felt the unexpected weight in his hands. Could he really be looking at a corm from the fabled *Heliamphora giganta*? It was undoubtedly an impressive item. About the size and shape of a pumpkin, it was glossy black with regular, deep grooves radiating from its base.

After a moment's silence, he placed it carefully back on the counter.

"Well, it seems to match the descriptions I found in the archive manuscripts of the Guild library. And of course the Venezuelan upland jungle is mentioned as a favoured habitat. But you must know that most authorities today deny the very existence of *Giganta*, or at least claim that it has been extinct for centuries." Jules tried his best to look suspicious. "I mean, had this fellow ever seen a specimen actually growing?"

The dealer made an impatient gesture with his hands. "Of course. There have been plenty of reports from that area. The Arawak fear it with deep superstition. According to Diego, it is known locally as *el comedor de mono*. The monkey eater."

"Isn't that a bit fanciful?" Jules stared at the inert bulk of the corm lying on the counter.

The dealer shrugged. "Indian folklore tells of fully-grown specimens trapping large animals, including inquisitive primates. It's entirely up to you whether you believe that or not."

He placed the corm back in its wooden box and closed the lid. "I must ask, Dr Finch, whether you have a genuine interest in purchase" he said, tapping the box with a forefinger. "There are other interested parties, you know."

"May I know who?" Jules asked, annoyed that his voice was betraying anxiety. Surely no one else from the Guild could have caught wind of this so soon?

"I'm afraid, professional discretion..." The dealer's voice trailed off and he turned both hands outwards, as if to imply regret.

"I'll take it" Jules said decisively, reaching into his jacket pocket. "I trust US dollars will be acceptable?"

★ ★ ★

The orangery, or plantarium as Jules called it, abutted the west wall of the house, overlooking a broad sweep of the South Downs countryside. A lofty affair of glass and ornate wrought iron, it was a Victorian addition to the property and had been the main reason why Jules had originally made the purchase. Indeed, it was the only thing that kept him there, since the house had become far too large for him now he lived alone. The children had left years ago and his wife's subsequent suicide was something he preferred not to talk about, even with the confiding Mrs Higgs who came in on weekdays to clean and cook.

Needless to say, she was not allowed in the plantarium. This was Jules' jealously-guarded inner sanctum, home to his precious collection of exotic and tropical plants. The airy space was filled by a wealth of tropical growth, reaching right up to the high glass domes of the roof. Bizarrely-shaped palms in giant plant pots jostled for place with exotic ferns, huge cacti and a bewildering array of flowering creepers hanging in brightly-coloured festoons. The effect was more than a little reminiscent of a Rousseau painting; one almost expected a tiger to leap out from behind the foliage.

Nearest the house wall were gathered Jules'

particular pride and joy, the insectivorous species – fly traps, pitcher plants and the like. Jules preferred to refer to them as carnivorous plants, something that amused and irritated other members of the Tropical Plant Guild.

"You really will have to stop using that term, you know Jules. I mean, dammit, insects aren't exactly meat, are they?"

But Jules was going to give those old fogeys good cause to eat their words. Before him, growing from his largest terracotta planter, rose the foliage of the legendary *Heliamphora giganta*. Admittedly, the mysterious corm purchased all those months ago had been a disappointment at first. After the initial excitement of planting it, using several sacks of his special marsh compost, Jules had come eagerly each morning to look for signs of life, but found none. Then, only a few weeks back, he had come in as usual one morning to find that a crown of pale, fleshy structures had erupted from the surface of the soil. They proceeded to grow upwards at an astonishing speed to form a circle of thick, cactus-like spines, bright blue-green in colour with razor-sharp yellow barbs along their outer edges.

Hardly daring to believe his fortune, Jules had watched day by day in amazement as these fat spines rapidly reached several feet in height, dominating everything else around them in the plantarium. But despite the impressive growth, something had seemed wrong. The plant lacked a pitcher or amphora, the leaf structure used by all the members of the genus *Heliamphora* to trap their prey.

Until a few days ago, that is. Then, with almost theatrical drama, the plant had produced a sudden surge of new central growth, forging its way upwards above the surrounding ring of spines to form a hollow tube, bulb-shaped at the base and flared outwards at the top. The appearance was similar to that of a giant *Sarraceria*, but much, much larger and with an exotic crown of long, curved hooks around the rim. Almost unbelievably, the whole structure was already two metres high and still growing.

Now Jules stood in his plantarium, looking up at this leviathan and laying his plans. The most important thing, of course, would be to reserve an entry place in the Guild's annual exotic species competition. The humiliation of last year's event still rang in his ears: "Look, I'm sorry, Jules old chap, I hate to disappoint. I mean, we all admire your enthusiasm for the insectivores and I'm sure this little fly trap is most unusual to someone such as yourself with specialised knowledge. But you must see that, in exotic terms, it hardly compares with entries like Harold's superb specimen of *Epidendrum nigra* s*plendiflora*, for example. The panel suggested that you might consider diversifying into other areas of special interest for next year."

Well, he would teach them to respect plant carnivores. His *giganta* was going to take the Guild by storm and carry off this year's prize. It was exotic all right, and of impressive size, too, no doubt about that. And now he would be able to silence all the sceptics who denied that such a species had ever existed.

Of course, the plant in its pot was already far too large to transport to the exhibition hall, but fortunately the Guild regulations allowed for this. Where specimens were over a certain size, the by-laws clearly stated that a sufficiently well-documented photographic entry was allowable. Jules had checked the member's handbook again only that morning.

But he would not reach too enthusiastically for his camera just yet. The extraordinary plant was clearly still developing, increasing not just in size but also in complexity of form and colour. It would be best to wait until it had reached full maturity before making a photographic record for the competition. Meanwhile, there was the intriguing prospect of testing the feeding capabilities of the plant.

Jules stopped musing. He removed his jacket and hung it over the back of a wicker chair. Then he rolled up his sleeves and gingerly removed the contents of the plastic bag he had just brought into the plantarium. In the absence of a monkey, the squirrel he had found in the road outside this morning would have to do. Holding the limp carcass by its tail, he pushed the wooden stepladder a little closer to *giganta*'s huge container and climbed up a couple of rungs, bringing his head level with the crown of the plant.

The sweet smell of over-ripe fruit which had been pervading the plantarium for several days hit him like a powerful drug. Part of the mechanism for attracting prey, Jules thought, just like the vivid red and green colours around the top of the plant's snare. He reached carefully between the long curved spines and gently edged the squirrel onto the rim of the amphora. The furry corpse slid over the edge and disappeared from view.

He was about to climb up further and peer inside when he saw a sudden spasm of movement around the crown. Then, with a clicking sound, the ring of spines flipped inwards, locking one with another across the top of the snare. Slightly unnerved, Jules quickly jumped down from the ladder and stepped back to watch. The trumpet-like top of the amphora had now constricted, with the bulk of the dead squirrel visible from the outside as a slight bulge about a third the way down. There followed a series of wave-like movements in the wall of the trap, apparently forcing the prey downwards into the bulb at the bottom.

Jules gazed in amazement. The trigger reaction of the spines was not unlike that seen in *Dionaea* species, the venus flytraps, but the contractions in the wall of the amphora were quite unexpected. They reminded him of the peristaltic movements visible in large constricting snakes after captured animals have been swallowed whole. There was clearly nothing passive about the way *giganta* handled its captives.

Following the feeding experiment, the central snare

of the plant remained constricted with the ring of spines locked across its rim for three whole days. Then on the fourth morning, Jules came into the plantarium to find the plant opened up again, the amphora returned to its previous shape and the ring of spines once more curving outwards from the crown. It was as if nothing had happened.

The plant continued to grow, relentlessly, day after day. Jules monitored it carefully, making detailed notes and starting to take preliminary photographs from the outside. In retrospect, he kicked himself for not having had the foresight to bring his camera and capture the squirrel episode. Perhaps that could be rectified later on, he thought.

★ ★ ★

"Not now, Mrs Higgs, can't you see I'm busy?"

Jules turned awkwardly to see his housekeeper's face peering round the half-open door leading into the house. The stepladder reached a long way up, and he was feeling decidedly insecure balanced on the top rung.

"Well I just wanted to remind you that it's my afternoon off, Dr Finch. I've left a cold supper in the fridge and there are some sandwiches in the pantry in case you get peckish at tea time." Her voice adopted a petulant note. "And I didn't mean to disturb you, I'm sure."

She had closed the door firmly behind her before Jules had time to reply. He turned cautiously back round on his perch to face the top of the astonishing plant. It had now reached a full three metres in height, its huge central amphora dwarfing the outer circle of fleshy, pointed leaves around its base. But in the last few days, growth appeared to have finally stopped.

Jules had chosen today to begin the process of making a detailed photographic study. But achieving good pictures of the inside of the amphora was proving difficult. Even at the very top of the ladder, he was only just level with the top of the plant and the crown of outward-curving spines were getting in his way. Moreover, the smell of over-ripe fruit had now become almost overpowering.

Gagging slightly, Jules leaned gingerly forward between two of the spines, craning his neck over the rim of the snare just far enough to peer down inside. It was an amazing sight. The interior was lined with bright yellow, cushion-like growth, increasingly streaked lurid red towards the bottom. A series of vertical grooves gave a ribbed, almost upholstered effect. Rather to Jules' surprise, there was no pool of digestive fluid in the base of the bulb, as was usual in Heliamphora species. Instead, the bottom of the trap was obscured by a carpet of bright red fronded structures, glistening with moisture, almost two meters below him. These possibly acted as a lure to prey, or even part of the plant's trigger mechanism, Jules thought.

He reached behind him and pulled his camera round over the rim of the amphora. Leaning over as far as he dared, he framed the view downwards and carefully adjusted the focus. At that moment, he felt a momentary tremor around the top of the amphora. It upset his precarious balance and he found himself half-lying on the flared rim. He kicked desperately backwards and found nothing but space. Seconds later there came an almighty crash from below as the stepladder hit the floor.

Legs flailing, Jules snatched at the fleshy growth inside the plant, dropping his camera as he did so. Aghast, he watched the camera land on the fronds in the base of the amphora.

He knew with a terrible certainty what would happen next. A series of much more powerful contractions began around the top of the amphora and then, horror of horrors, he felt himself squeezed inexorably downwards, head first, into the stinking snare. Blind with terror, Jules felt the large spines around the rim of the plant flip over and lock around his buttocks, pushing him further into the plant's interior. The stench was suffocating. His face was smothered by the cushion-like surfaces as they contracted around him. The ring of spines locked above him. Soft, moist darkness merged into oblivion.

It would be some time before *Heliamphora giganta* would need to feed again.

BETRAYAL

The limousine moved silently past below, black and opulent. Marcus monitored its progress from his vantage point at the top of the cedar tree, high enough to see the entrance drive all the way from the main park gates up to the big house. After stopping in front of the grand front portico, the chauffeur got out and held open one of the passenger doors.

Marcus watched as Lady Marchant and her daughter climbed up the stone steps to the front door. Almost at once a servant emerged from the doorway, bustling forward to help them with their brightly-coloured bags and packages. Marcus could not hear the sounds of lively voices and clattering high heels, nor the crunching of gravel as the car drove off around the back of the house, but he knew that mother and daughter had been out shopping together. Wednesday was the usual day for shopping expeditions and he had seen them leave as usual that morning. It was hot again today and Suzanna was wearing a summer dress which showed off her figure in a way that fiercely aroused him. His eyes followed every sway of her hips until the front door closed behind them.

Just then, something hard hit him on the cheek. Looking down, he saw his sister Celia on the ground below, about to hurl another cedar cone up at him. She was calling out, but she was too far away for him to make out what she was saying. With familiar ease, Marcus shinned down the huge tree, picked up another cone from the ground and narrowly missed her with a return throw. She ducked and turned back towards him, looking annoyed. He watched her lips carefully as she shouted across at him.

"Stop that, you idiot! Dad sent me to get you. He's clearing the dead oak by the lake and you're to go and give him a hand at once!"

Marcus scowled and gave a mock salute before loping off across the park in the direction of the lake. A few years ago, he would have made a flying tackle with the intention of wrestling his sister to the ground, but these days she seemed to have lost interest in that kind of thing and would only have told him to behave himself and grow up. A pity, really, because fighting together had forged a bond between them when they were both younger, at least partly making up for not being able to talk together. He was being given speech lessons at the deaf school, but back home he had stubbornly refused to put them into practice, fearing that his efforts would sound grotesque to anyone who could hear them. And in a way, remaining mute suited him. After all, his own world was entirely without sound, so it seemed somehow right that he should be soundless himself. It didn't really bother him any longer, this cocoon of silence he lived in. It helped him to feel alone with his surroundings, so his life felt somehow secret, something just for him. If he did not like what someone was saying, all he had to do was look away and it was as if they were not there at all. His father understood that, Marcus thought, but not his sister, these days.

Emerging from the shrubbery surrounding the lake, he spotted his father now, waving from the side of the stricken oak tree, piles of fallen branches already stacked beside its shattered stump. Perhaps he would be allowed to use the big felling axe. He would enjoy that.

* * *

The heat was oppressive and Marcus wiped sweat from his face, steadying himself against the top of the orchard wall. From here he had an uninterrupted view of the gardens at the back of the house, including the terrace where Suzanna was sunbathing in a bikini. It was the first time he had seen her like that and the sight was both mesmerising and strangely disturbing. As she rolled over onto her back, displaying her barely-concealed breasts, he felt himself go hard with desire, the blood pounding between his temples. He would have given anything to be able to touch her near-naked body, to feel the softness of her skin. But such lustful thoughts also brought a conflict of shame and embarrassment. She was forbidden fruit, a creature from a different world, living in a society beyond his reach. Even a chance encounter would surely be humiliating and unthinkable.

A sudden itching over his knees finally broke the spell and he looked down to see an army of ants swarming off the warm brickwork onto the bare skin of his legs. Brushing them off irritably, he dropped silently down to the ground and walked back through the fruit trees to the door in the orchard wall. Once outside, he carefully locked the door again and returned the key to its customary hiding place under a large stone. He was in the mood to go back to his room and continue his fantasies in peace.

The groundsman's cottage was in a far corner of the park, half hidden by a copse of beech trees near to the gate that lead out to the village. The cottage had only two upstairs rooms. Not long after their mother's death Celia had moved a bed down into the front parlour, claiming that space for herself. She had been insistent that she was old enough to need a room of her own and could not be expected to go on sharing with a younger brother. Marcus found no cause to complain; it was an opportunity to have the bedroom to himself. Indeed, the prospect of complete privacy had suddenly seemed attractive.

Arriving now to find no one at home, he clambered up the rickety wooden staircase, closed his door behind him and just to be sure, wedged the latch with its peg. Then he reached under a loose floorboard and pulled out his stash of magazines, discreetly salvaged from the heaps of rubbish put out for collection when Viscount Moorlake, Suzanna's brother, had gone up to Oxford the previous autumn. They were, Marcus had realised at once, very much adult magazines and more than fascinating enough for him to risk smuggling them into his room.

Lying back on his bed, he turned the pages of one of these trophies until he came to a full-page photograph of a sparsely-clad, nubile young woman in a suggestive pose. Marcus found this picture particularly erotic, and only allowed himself the luxury of studying it on special occasions. Such as now, for instance.

The effects were reliable and swift, leading to a surge of lust and a hard erection. Guiltily, but unable to restrain himself, Marcus reached a hand down to help the rising tide of pleasure onwards to its final brief stab of ecstasy. It was all over in minutes: a compelling and yet disappointing act, which left behind nothing except a damp patch and a vague feeling of remorse. Not for the first time, he couldn't help feeling that there should be more to it than this. He lay staring at the picture again, wondering what it would be like to do it with a real, live woman.

Just at that moment, he felt the floor shaking: the familiar warning of someone climbing the stairs. He barely had time to push the magazines back into hiding before looking up to see the door latch being jolted up and down from the outside. Removing the wedge, he pulled open the door to be confronted by his sister, her face mouthing ill-concealed irritation.

"So this is where you're hiding out then? Dad and I've been looking everywhere for you. Supper's been on the table for ages and no thanks to you. Some of us pull our weight around here you know!"

Marcus turned away and shrugged his shoulders, not wishing to see any more of his sister's diatribe. There was little rapport between them these days and he did not like the way Celia had changed as she got older. From being a bit of a playful tomboy, someone you could have fun with, she had turned into a bossy and aloof older-brother figure. Certainly no substitute for the mother they didn't have any longer. Resentment boiled up for a moment, but he followed her down the stairs all the same, hunger overcoming his pride.

★ ★ ★

The guests had been arriving all morning, their smart cars now drawn up in rows in front of the house, glistening in the heat of the midday sun. Even Viscount Moorlake had come back from Oxford for the event, driving his bright red sports tourer. It was pretty stylish, Marcus thought, although cars had never really excited him that much.

Earlier in the day, a long table had been carried out onto the veranda at the rear of the house and laid up for lunch, so it had been clear that the party would be outside. He had been watching them over the top of the orchard wall for over two hours now, imagining the sounds of their laughing voices, the clatter of plates, the popping of champagne corks. They were, he thought, fashionable and beautiful people, brimming over with confidence and privilege, apparently without a care in the world.

Yet increasingly, as the afternoon wore on, Marcus began to feel resentment at the gulf between their lives and his own, almost as if he were being deliberately excluded from their party rather than secretly spying on it.

Suzanna was there, of course, and that was what had drawn him to watch in the first place. Today she seemed perfect, glamorously dressed and more achingly gorgeous than ever. The trouble was, some of the male guests obviously felt the same way, judging by the attentions she had been receiving. As time wore on, Marcus had become increasingly agitated by the more obvious flirting directed at Suzanna and unable to stem the tide of anger and jealousy rising inside himself.

Towards the end of the meal, the guests began circulating freely around the table, breaking up into smaller groups out on the veranda, still smoking and drinking. It was at this stage that one particular young man approached Suzanna and started behaving in a very familiar fashion, at one point even putting his arm around her and spinning her around in a mock pirouette. Marcus was relieved to see that Suzanna appeared less than pleased by this, but it was still all he could do to restrain himself from jumping over the wall and rushing up to deal the man a swift right hook.

Finally he could not bear to watch any longer and dropped back down into the orchard. He sat for a while on the scorched ground with his back to the wall, taking slow breaths and letting the warmth of the sun soak into his body. After a while, his feelings of outrage lessened and a sense of his own ridiculousness rose up to taunt him. He started to weep silently, filled with frustration and humiliation, clenching his fists and grinding them into his eyes. Eventually, he decided to seek solace in the only way which seemed to offer genuine escape. Getting to his feet, he left the orchard and headed back to the cottage. His bedroom was an airless furnace in the heat, but that suited him in his present state. He wedged the door latch carefully and reached under the loose floorboard.

★ ★ ★

The iron jaws of the gin trap were sprung shut, but it was without prey. Whatever had stolen the bait had not got away unscathed, Marcus noticed. There was fresh blood on the metalwork. He carefully reset the mechanism, raking over dead leaves as camouflage. It was disappointing, but he still had the traps behind the temple to inspect. Perhaps they would prove more rewarding. This was his last day of freedom before school started and today of all days he was hoping to find a kill.

As he knelt, a violent tremor through the ground

alerted him to thunder, a silent sensation familiar from past experience. It was not a surprise. The afternoon had gradually become increasingly sultry and oppressive, with slowly-building mountains of cloud threatening a violent end to the heatwave. Now as he stood up, Marcus felt the first heavy drops of warm rain on the back of his neck. The storm built with alarming rapidity and he only just had time to find shelter under a nearby clump of giant rhododendron bushes before the deluge started in earnest. Sheets of water bounced off the parched ground. Foliage was buffeted by squalls of wind and the daylight dwindled to near darkness, pierced at intervals by forks of lightning. Nature's anger held sway.

As Marcus peered out from his shelter, he became aware of someone scurrying across the open ground beyond, perhaps a hundred yards distant. It was a woman, soaked to the skin with long wet hair plastered down over her head and shoulders, but unmistakably it was the figure of Suzanna. Her sodden red dress clung tightly to her body and as he watched her move, Marcus once again felt stirrings of lust arising unbidden within him. But there was also a sense of amazement that she should be out in such weather and so far from the house.

As far as he could make out, she was heading in the direction of the temple. Perhaps she was seeking shelter there, he thought. After she had moved out of sight, he abandoned the refuge of his bushes and ran towards the woodland behind, feeling the full force of the downpour as he did so. Now soaking wet himself, but driven by an irresistible urge to find out what Suzanna would do next, he worked his way around the edge of the cover afforded by the trees, trying to catch another glimpse of her red dress in the drenched and gloomy landscape beyond.

Suddenly a particularly bright lightning flash lit up the dome of the temple, set against the dark line of trees in the middle distance. For a brief instant he saw not only a flash of red inside its semicircle of pillars but the outline of a second figure alongside.

Marcus moved along the margin of the woodland to get as close as he dared and then peered out from behind the trunk of a large beech tree. He was barely a stone's throw from the temple plinth, but the branches of the tree were bent low enough to offer concealment, even at this distance.

For a moment the downpour eased slightly. Looking between the pillars he could clearly see Suzanna; but there was someone with her. A darkly-clad figure was holding her in an intimate embrace under the centre of the dome. Their faces were pressed together in a long and passionate kiss. When they eventually pulled apart they were at first facing away from him, but then the dark figure turned.

Recognition fell on Marcus with sudden and terrible certainty. It was the face of Celia, his sister. He stared, uncomprehending for an instant, and then was engulfed by an overwhelming sense of outrage. Uppermost in his emotional turmoil was a sense of betrayal: by Suzanna and his own sister, yes, but also by his own emotions, the secret feelings which seemed suddenly to have led him so badly astray.

As the storm renewed its intensity, he felt his whole body convulse, his lungs finally forcing out a bloodcurdling, banshee wail of despair. It was the first real sound Marcus had made in weeks, but no one heard it; his cry was drowned out by a monumental clap of thunder, like a judgement from on high. Marcus's flight from the temple went entirely unnoticed, his agony and despair drowned out by the tempest.

DRAGON BUTTRESS

"Safe!"

David's disembodied voice echoed down from higher up the cliff face, to be quickly answered by the screeching alarm calls of birds in the trees below. Breathing an inward sigh of relief, Alex slipped the rope out of his belay device and shouted back up to his friend, hoping his voice would also carry far enough.

"Off belay!"

His call sounded strangely small, swamped by the scale and grandeur of the landscape. But David must have heard him, because the rope began to pull upwards over the rock buttress, snaking out of the neatly-coiled slack at Alex's feet, feet that were going numb after nearly an hour of inactivity on the narrow ledge of the first belay point.

Alex wriggled his toes again and gently rolled his shoulders to try to release the tension that had built up during the long wait. On both sides, the massive cliffs of the Ruthstein fault stretched away like a great curtain wall, rising majestically above the jungle canopy of the rift valley. Their camp site, reached by a sweaty two-day trek, was hidden by the roof of dense foliage lying below. It had been wonderful to emerge from the trees into bright sunshine half way up the first pitch, leaving the humidity and biting insects behind.

And what a view had unfolded. Magnificent rock scenery which sent the blood racing, with scores of climbing routes beckoning in every direction. But it had been the Dragon Buttress which had drawn them all the way here; the daunting and magnificent rock spur that now soared above Alex's head. Until now, no one had been successful in pioneering a route up the buttress. All previous attempts had been defeated by a giant overhanging section on the second pitch. By mutual consent, David had led this crux point of the route, since he was the more agile climber of the two.

Alex had watched him with considerable anxiety as he edged up the overhang from their first belay. The climbing clearly involved moves which would take skill and nerve, even when seconding with protection in place. Moreover, the long wait after David had disappeared from view hinted at more challenges further up the pitch. But at least they now had a safe belay point above the crux. Perhaps they really could complete a first ascent of the infamous Dragon Buttress.

By now, the remaining rope had all been pulled up. Alex could imagine David putting the finishing touches to his belay point out of sight above. At long last it was time for him to turn the apprehension of his long wait into action. The overhang beckoned above.

"Climb when ready!"

David's call was faint, but it sounded reassuringly measured. Laid back, even. He had nerves of steel, that man, Alex thought, not for the first time. He dismantled his own protection and waited until the final slack was taken in, so the rope was just taut to his harness. It was time to go.

"Climbing!"

Alex's upward call did not sound as calm as he had intended, but after the first few moves, his confidence started to return again. Pausing only to remove David's well-spaced nuts and friends from their rock crevices, he swung out below the overhang, his hands instinctively finding a succession of surprisingly reassuring holds.

This was not so bad after all. David was keeping the rope nicely tight and his nerves were rapidly settling. Finally, he was able to ease his body around the outer edge of the overhang and look up to see the continuation of the pitch. David had chosen to follow a long vertical fissure just to one side of the main prow of the buttress. At the top of this crack the rope disappeared, seemingly over the lip of a wide ledge. Although David was not visible, Alex assumed that the next belay was back from the ledge, behind his sight line. He removed a slightly recalcitrant nut from a small crack just above his head, stowed the quick draw on his harness and reached up for the next hold, a promising-looking pocket in the rock surface.

Just then the peacefulness of the crag was broken by a sudden commotion coming from above.

"Bloody hell! Oh my god... get off, you bastard!"

David's distant shouts were accompanied by the sounds of a struggle and also by an odd bellowing sound which Alex could not identify. Then everything began to happen very quickly.

"Below! Alex, look out!"

There was a further loud cry from David, then a heavy thud and the ominous rattle of loose stones cascading down the cliff face. For a second Alex froze in horror, instinctively hugging the rock and tucking his face downwards beneath his helmet. The rocks crashed past, missing him by what felt like inches. They were accompanied by a large, bulky form, limbs flailing, which emitted an unearthly, high-pitched wail as it disappeared below and crashed through the roof of the jungle foliage. The sound of breaking branches was joined by a cacophony of clattering and screaming from the wildlife below.

Then silence.

Alex's mind raced, his heart pounding. Whatever had fallen with the loose rocks, it had not been David. It hadn't even been human. Despite the moment of near panic, he had clearly seen a large, thrashing tail as the creature plummeted past him.

"David! Are you OK?" he yelled. There was no answer but the mocking echo of his own voice.

If it hadn't been David who had fallen, he must still

be up on the ledge, but somehow hurt or senseless. What the bloody hell was he going to do?

The rope had now gone slack, redundant loops slowly sliding down from the rock ledge above. Alex peered up, anxiously looking for signs of life, and was suddenly astonished to see the head of a huge lizard poking out from the ledge, its pointed muzzle and flicking tongue framed by an angry ruff of quivering green scales. A second later it retreated backwards and vanished from sight.

Alex thought back to their inward trek through the rift valley. More than once, local villagers had told them stories of colonies of giant lizards – monitor lizards, they sounded like - living high on the cliff face. They claimed that this was how the buttress had come by its name. At the time, such tales had seemed just too improbable, merely the stuff of folklore.

Not any more.

"David! For Christ's sake say something! Are you hurt?"

Alex's call echoed round the rock face, but it was followed by silence. Fighting back panic, he told himself to stay calm and think. There had to be something he could do. Not down-climbing from his current position. That was just too risky, especially with the huge overhang below. Anyway, he couldn't be sure how much slack rope there would be. Almost certainly not enough, depending on what was going on at the belay above. Most importantly, it was unthinkable just to abandon his friend up there, possibly alive and hurt. There was really only one sensible course: to continue free climbing upwards to the ledge without top rope protection.

Alex swallowed hard. Already his hands were numb in their holds, his arms aching from holding a static pose. It had to be done quickly, or his muscles would get pumped.

Trying not to think about the consequences of coming off, he started to move up the rock crack, slack coils of rope hanging uselessly between his legs. Balancing precariously from one move to the next, he unclipped the rope as he passed each protection point, leaving valuable equipment hanging from the rock in his haste. It served no practical purpose now and could only snare the rope.

The climb seemed to last an eternity, but the holds kept coming; David had chosen the route well. Finally, with a bit of insecure foot-smearing against the rock face as the crack finally petered out, Alex levered himself up so his head was above the level of the ledge, his hands groping for unseen holds just over the lip.

In a few brief seconds he took in the scene that lay before him. The ledge was actually a huge horizontal fault line in the cliffs, forming a broad rock shelf. Alex at once saw the body of his friend on the floor of the shelf, face down amongst a tangle of rope and climbing equipment.

"David? Hang on, I'm coming!" Alex shouted, in a mixture of panic and dismay.

He hauled himself up onto the flat surface of the rock shelf and rolled David's limp form over. His friend's features were blue and swollen, tongue protruding, eyelids puffed up so that his face was beyond recognition. One of his trouser legs was torn and soaked in blood. There were several gaping puncture marks in his mutilated left calf.

A quick examination revealed no sign of breath or pulse. The giant lizard, if that was what had attacked him, had obviously been fatally venomous.

Scarcely able to believe what was happening, Alex stood up. A finger of fear crept down his spine as he took in his awful predicament. Could there possibly be a way out of this disaster? He looked rapidly around, taking in his surroundings in more detail. Immediately to his right, the rock shelf disappeared from sight around the jutting prow of the buttress. Beyond this, it was clearly visible again, snaking like a terrace across the cliff face as far as the eye could see. In the far distance, the shelf line seemed to connect with a series of huge caves in the cliff face - fascinating and quite unexpected, but not offering an obvious escape route. Immediately above him, the sheer rock of the buttress towered on upwards, impossibly forbidding. How had they ever thought it could be climbed?

Alex turned back to look at the belay that David had fixed before disaster struck. There was no way he could get his friend's body down single handed, but he could perhaps rig up an unsecured abseil for himself. There might just be enough rope to get all the way past the overhang down to the jungle floor.

Fighting back panic, he had just knelt to start untangling the rope when a grunting sound stopped him dead in his tracks. He whipped round, to find himself confronted with the head of a great lizard, looking at him from behind a rock at eye level. It was barely twenty feet away.

Alex jumped up in terror. As he did so, the beast advanced round the corner of the buttress into full view, its head swaying from side to side in a menacing fashion. It was huge, the size of a large alligator at least, but more massively built. Gobs of sticky saliva drooled from its jaws. The ruff of skin around its neck swelled, pulsating slightly. A nauseous, fetid stench swept over the ledge. Alex moved cautiously backwards, wishing he had some sort of weapon, almost overcome by a sense of isolation and overwhelming fear.

Now the head of a second, slightly smaller lizard had appeared around the corner from behind, raising its long neck and emitting an odd bellowing sound. As if this were a signal, the larger beast suddenly reared forwards, its jaws open wide. There was too little room to manoeuvre, for everything was overpoweringly close. Alex tried to sidestep the lunging attack, but his foot caught in the coils of rope. He lost his balance and fell backwards into the void, arms clutching uselessly into thin air.

The descent seemed to last forever. At first he was

falling freely through the air, his mind racing with terror and helplessness. Then, inevitably, his flailing body crashed into the rocks, a hip, then an elbow, seared with pain. He bounced back into space again.

Just as Alex was convinced his last moment had come, the rope went suddenly tight: snagged perhaps, or simply run full out from the top belay. His harness cut up under his rib cage with a jolt that squeezed all the breath from his body.

All downward movement had ceased. Alex was now hanging upside down, just below the jutting promontory of the overhang, spiralling round and round, battered, terrified and barely conscious. A couple of small rocks fell past, dislodged by his fall. Agonising seconds later, he heard them crashing through the jungle canopy far below.

After a few minutes he managed to lever himself upright, wincing in discomfort at the pain in his rib cage and left hip. Perhaps he could reach the cliff face. He tried to swing himself inwards, aiming to get close enough to grab at the rock under the overhang. But it was too far away and eventually he abandoned the struggle, overcome by exhaustion.

Time passed, unmeasured. Jungle life echoed up above the tree cover. Parrots screeched, a howler monkey boomed. A curious numbness crept over Alex's body, taking him beyond feelings of pain and despair. Finally, as the daylight began to fade from the forest, hope ebbed away into blackness and oblivion.

VERMIN

"I bet he's got stuff in there," Lurch said, peering out from behind the heap of rubble.

Will did not know why his friend was called Lurch, just that everyone addressed him as that. Actually, Will was not supposed to be out with Lurch at all. His parents did not approve of him or his family. They lived in an area of run-down council housing which had something of a reputation for crime and violence. Or so Will's father maintained. But there was undoubtedly something exciting about being out with Lurch. Despite being small, scrawny and generally not much to look at, he somehow managed to command admiration and respect from all the other boys on the estate.

Not the girls, of course. They never, any of them, associated with girls.

"What do you mean, stuff?" Will replied, as they stared out across the derelict area beyond their vantage point. In the distance stood the object of their surveillance: a tottering end-of-terrace house, its exposed wall propped up by huge wooden beams.

"You know" Lurch said. "Stuff. Cash in the teapot. That kind of thing."

As usual, they were waiting for a sighting of Grandpa Fox, nicknamed on account of his seemingly immense age and long, gingery moustache. Grandpa Fox had been staked out for several days now and they were getting to know his habits. This afternoon, they watched as he emerged from the back door of his house at the end of the terrace, carefully locking it and looking warily around him before setting off. He moved slowly and rather unsteadily across the rubble-strewn wasteland to the end of the surfaced road, then more purposefully along what remained of the pavement.

"I reckon you could get in through that little window above the yard wall," Lurch said. "Get in real easy."

To Will it looked anything but easy. "What if he comes back sooner than last time?" he said.

"You chickening out, or what?" Lurch replied scornfully. "I can always find someone else to do it with. I don't need you if you're going yellow."

Will said nothing. He would never live the humiliation down, he knew. It was something of an honour for him to be taken into Lurch's confidence, and not one he was prepared to throw up, despite his nagging scruples.

Once Grandpa Fox was safely out of sight, the two boys set off across the wasteland, crouching down and using short bursts of stealthy, weaving movement, just as people did in the movies. There was no one to see them, but that was not the point.

Grandpa Fox's house was not the only one left in the

decaying terrace, but it was the only one still being lived in. For some months now, he had stubbornly resisted the Council's eviction order, despite the almost continuous demolition going on all around him. The area had now acquired an atmosphere of dereliction, remote from the inhabited houses further up the road.

There was a real sense of adventure as Will and Lurch reached the heavily-strutted end wall of the house. It was a simple matter to climb up one of the timber props onto the wall surrounding the back yard, although Will eyed the row of glass shards running along the top edge with apprehension. Once at the top they dropped over the other side, landing on the roof of a coal bunker. Will paused to stare at the extraordinary collection of junk filling the back yard: old bicycles, an upturned bath, a rusting washing machine, endless fragments of unidentifiable machinery, all quietly rusting away amongst the few remaining patches of lank grass.

"Come on," Lurch whispered, "give us a hand, will you?"

In the event, the small window above the coal bunker yielded easily. Its wooden frame was largely rotten, the catch inside hanging on by a single remaining screw. Wriggling through, Will dropped down after Lurch into a small cloakroom, which smelled of stale urine and contained only a lidless lavatory bowl and a pile of old newspapers. Not even any bog roll, Will noticed.

They emerged from the toilet into what seemed to be the main living room, dimly lit through a front window hung with dirty net curtains. The space was mostly occupied by two sagging old sofas and more heaps of old newspapers.

A pale shape darted out from under one of the sofas and disappeared through a far door, causing Will to start violently.

"Only a cat, silly," said Lurch, with impressive self-control.

One wall of the room was taken up by an open-plan staircase. On the other was a disused fireplace.

"Shit!" Lurch yelped, all the whispering suddenly forgotten. "What the fuck is that?"

Will followed his gaze, hearing the alarm in Lurch's voice. Suspended from a cord stretched in front of the fireplace there were three large animals, clearly dead, all matted in dried blood and hanging by their tails. One of them appeared to be missing its head.

"They're miles too big for mice," Will said, backing slightly further away in revulsion. "Do you suppose they could be rats, or what?"

"Bloody pervert," Lurch said, passing over his ignorance of the animal kingdom. "I bet he gets a kick out of torturing animals."

He turned and disappeared for a moment into the tiny kitchen, while Will continued to stare, horrified, at the mutilated, dangling corpses.

"Nothing in there 'cept cat food and dirty dishes,"

Lurch reported. In fact, there hadn't even been a teapot, let alone any cash in it.

"I reckon we ought to get out of here," Will said, by now fully unnerved by events. "He could come back any time."

"Well I'm going to have a poke around up them stairs," Lurch replied. "There might be money under a mattress or something. You can never tell. 'Course, I don't need you if you're not up for it."

The calculated insult stung Will's pride and he followed Lurch warily up the stairs, quietly wishing he had never embarked on this escapade in the first place. And then his worst fears were realised. They had barely reached the landing when they heard the unmistakeable sound of a latch key and a door opening coming from downstairs. Simultaneously, there was a spine-chilling screech from the cat.

The two boys stopped dead in their tracks and turned to look at each other, soundlessly, alarm mirrored in each of their faces. Almost at once, Grandpa Fox appeared in the kitchen doorway and turned to look up the staircase. It was as if he expected to find them there.

"Vermin!" he yelled. "Filthy vermin! I'll get you!"

With a surprisingly deft movement for an old man, he reached behind the kitchen door. Before either of the boys could move or speak, they found themselves looking down the twin barrels of a shotgun.

"Christ! He's got a gun!" screeched Will. "Quick, in

here!" Without pausing to look round, he pushed a petrified Lurch into the room immediately behind them and slammed the door. Then came the sound of heavy footfalls ascending the stairs, almost drowned out by another threatening roar. "Filthy vermin!" bellowed Grandpa Fox. Heavy panting sounds could be heard through the door, followed by thumping steps across the landing floor.

"I knows what to do with vermin! I'll kill you!" shouted the old man.

Surprising himself with his own presence of mind, Will saw a key on the inside of the door and turned it. Seconds later, the door handle was rattled furiously and the door was kicked hard from the outside.

"Get away from the door, you idiot!" Will whispered, pulling the still-terrified Lurch back into a far corner of the room.

"I'll 'ave you! Just you see!"

There was a metallic clicking noise just outside the door, then an ear-splitting bang and the sound of splintering wood. Huge wooden shards flew across the room, followed by wreaths of acrid smoke. Momentarily deafened by the blast, the two boys stared in horror at the gaping rent in the door and the debris strewn out in front of them on the floor. Then, unexpectedly, there came an eerie, high-pitched cry, almost like someone choking. Almost immediately there was a loud crash, followed by a series of heavy thudding sounds and then, finally, silence.

It was a silence that seemed to go on forever, through the fading light and into almost complete darkness. Suddenly, Will could bear it no longer. He nudged the mute, crouching shape of Lurch, dimly visible next to him.

"I'm not staying here all night," he whispered. "I'm getting out of here. Are you coming or what?"

There was no response beyond a whimpering noise as Lurch's shadowy form retreated further back across the room. Surprised by his own audacity and despite a barely-contained sense of panic, Will approached the door, turned the key and slowly heaved the splintered wood open on bent hinges. There was just enough light still coming from the downstairs windows to confirm that there was no one on the landing or the stairs.

Lurch was clearly a lost cause. Will swallowed hard and determined to make a dash for it. Barely aware of what he was doing, he rushed out and tore down the staircase, across the living room and out through the open kitchen door into the night. There was no time to look at the crumpled, strangely distorted human form lying just beyond the foot of the stairs.

★ ★ ★

"It says here that old Mr Brent's been found dead." Will's father looked up from the newspaper and shook his head. "I guess they'll be able to get on and finish bulldozing those last few slums now."

"Does it say what he died of?" his mother asked from across the breakfast table. "Not that I'm sorry to hear it. He had dirty habits and lived in terrible squalour, by all accounts."

"Heart attack, apparently, collapsed at the bottom of his stairs. But it says here that he'd been killing vermin with a shotgun and stringing them up in his own living room."

"Well, there you are," Will's mother retorted. "What a terrible way to carry on. I always said he wasn't right in the head."

"Can't say I blame him about them vermin, though," Will's father said. "They had them in the next door's garden you know, and the council never lifted a finger."

Silent until now behind his cereal bowl, eyes growing wider by the minute, Will could contain himself no longer.

"Mum, what's vermin?" he finally blurted out.

"Just nasty things, dear," said his mother, "that carry diseases and need poison put down."

"Waste of time, that," Will's father interrupted. "They just need shooting, I reckon. I'm with old Mr Brent on that."

Rather more unnerved than he cared to admit, Will slid down from the table. Picking up his school satchel and sports kit in the hall, he decided that he wasn't going to take any chances about the affair. He had no idea what had become of Lurch that terrible evening, but for his own part he knew he'd had a very lucky escape. As he let himself out of the front door and set off down the garden path to the bus stop, he determined never to have anything more to do with Lurch or any of his cronies. He did not want to be called vermin ever again. By anyone.

BIN 44

These days I mostly drink cheap New World wine from supermarkets, but for years I used to buy the good stuff, lots of it. Ever since joining the Wine Circle at university I had been fascinated by the world of top-class vintage wine. Over the years it had become more than just a hobby; almost an obsession.

Vintage claret was my thing and in particular, the best châteaux of Graves. Until quite recently I was regularly to be found at wine auctions, shippers' warehouses and private tastings, usually speculating on younger, undisclosed vintages and buying by the case. But I also spent some time pursuing older wine and I would often pay large sums for rare single bottles from some of the most celebrated years of the century.

I should emphasise that I was not one of these people who use fine wine only as a speculative investment, buying and storing merely to sell on as a profit-making exercise. OK, I did a little of that, but in the main I was interested in actually drinking the stuff. I regularly organised wine-tasting parties for personal friends, some of whom dated back to my time at university. Looking back now, I think it would be fair to say that for many years I was spending a disproportionate amount of my disposable income in this way. But I had no dependants and was following a lucrative professional career in investment banking, so I never remember feeling guilty in the least.

Then came the Haut Brion fiasco, as I now think of it, and everything changed.

I suppose it really started on the evening of the annual University Wine Circle reunion. I should explain that this rather exclusive society had been formed during my undergraduate years and had long since ceased active recruitment. Although the number of surviving members had diminished considerably, a hardcore of enthusiasts continued to keep in touch, meeting once a year in restaurants known for their cellars. It was a tradition that each attending member chose (and paid for) one bottle from the wine list to accompany the meal. On this occasion, we had booked one of those wonderful Dickensian institutions which retain the tradition of having private dining rooms. There was now an open restaurant area on the ground floor, but the old rooms upstairs were still available for private hire to those in the know. They were reached by a labyrinth of narrow stairways and corridors that could not have changed for a century.

The plush cosiness of the room we occupied that night suited our needs well, since we always valued privacy when sharing and discussing fine wine. As ever, the discussion around the table was both lively and informed, continuing well into the night. Eventually, the table was cleared of the last remnants of the meal, leaving only the bottles, decanters and glasses glinting in the candlelight.

Soon afterwards, I remember becoming aware of an interesting discussion taking place at the other end of the table concerning the legacy of the phylloxera aphid. As you will no doubt know, this terrible pest ravaged the vineyards of northern Europe towards the end of the nineteenth century, eventually destroying all the vines of the great French vineyards. The disaster was overcome only by large-scale replanting and grafting onto resistant American rootstock. There are different opinions about the outcome of this, but since most people alive today have never tasted pre-phylloxera wine, comparison with the vintages that followed the replanting is now mostly speculative.

On the evening in question, Andrew Hammersmith, a particular friend of mine, was giving his opinion that no subsequent vintages, even from the truly great French châteaux, are ever likely to have attained the depth and quality yielded by the old vines. I had heard the argument many times before and knew Andrew's views, but what caught my attention that night was his assertion that he knew a cellar which might still harbour some remaining bottles from pre-phylloxera vine stock. Although pressed on the matter by some of the others sitting close by, I remember he had been very reluctant to go into detail and the conversation soon passed on to other topics.

It must have been about two days later that Andrew telephoned me.

"David? It's Andrew – Andrew Hammersmith. Listen, I wonder if you'd be interested in a private wine auction? It's rather a special affair, actually, a large cellar of vintage stuff. It's being offered up for complete clearance. Invitation only and all that, but I've managed to swing a couple of tickets via a family contact. I wondered whether you'd like to come along?"

Would I like to come? A silly question. Damn right I would.

So the following week found us driving together up to the Midlands, eagerly discussing what we might find in the way of vintage rarities. The cellar apparently belonged to an aristocratic family which had latterly fallen on hard times and was in need of capital. Andrew had been told that the collection had been built up over several generations and that the contents had been drunk only sparingly by the family members in more recent years. It all sounded very promising indeed.

The house itself was a grand, neoclassical affair set in extensive parkland and kept well out of the public eye. On our arrival we were immediately ushered through a side door out of the great hallway, down steep stone steps and into the underground cellars where the auction was to be held. We entered a very extensive, brick-vaulted space, rather dimly lit by bare electric light bulbs hanging from exposed wiring which was festooned with cobwebs.

The wines were stored towards one end, some in stacks of wooden cases, others as individual bottles on racks. The adjacent area had been cleared to allow for a few rows of plastic chairs, which had been arranged facing a long, low table covered by a white cloth. As expected, the auction was a very exclusive event and I recognised none of the twenty or so other people present. Amongst these were a small number of official-looking men, apparently staff hired from a specialist auctioneering firm.

Disappointingly, if perhaps not surprisingly, it soon became apparent that this was not one of those events where prior tasting is planned. The auction began soon after we arrived.

The proceedings were brisk and professional, and were conducted in near silence with the exception of the announcement of each successive lot. The bins on offer were small, usually no more than a case or two each, but all the wines were of considerable quality. Fabulous vintages from top French châteaux followed one after another, veritable giants of the world of claret.

Despite this, the bidding was both brisk and confident. Such large sums of money were changing hands and so rapidly that I was pretty sure most of the bidders were dealers. However, Andrew and I both had quite extensive previous experience of private wine auctions and within the first half hour or so we each managed to bid successfully, within a reasonable budget, for cases of *petits châteaux* from fine vintages. I remember being particularly pleased with the acquisition of a case of 1976 Château Cissac. I would have dearly liked to have managed some of the more prestigious names on offer, but the final bidding prices for most of these were frankly daunting, even for me.

Then came Bin 44. I shall never forget the number. Bin 44 was clearly something unusual from the moment it was announced. For a start, it was a single bottle, a magnum in fact. And secondly, we were all invited to come forward and examine it on the auctioneers' table before bidding began. Only a handful of people took advantage of this; presumably single bottles were of little interest to most of the professional dealers present.

The wine was Haut Brion, the one and only great *premier cru* of Graves, which in itself had my heart racing. But the date on the peeling and mildew-spotted label was frankly awe-inspiring. This fabulous bottle was from one of the greatest vintages ever recorded towards the tail end of the nineteenth century and almost certainly from pre-phylloxera vine stock. It was over one hundred years old.

Andrew exchanged a knowing glance with me and we retired to our seats again in silence. But I knew I had to have that bottle. The opportunity of tasting a truly great claret from the lost era of vinification would be a once-in-a-lifetime experience and for that, I was prepared to pay.

The bidding was opened at £500 and at first I held back, aiming to try and assess the degree of interest. As far as I could gather, only three people were placing bids to start with, although things were moving very quickly and with great discretion. Once the bidding price reached four figures, as I had assumed it would, one of the other interested parties dropped out and I cautiously motioned with my hand to enter the fray.

After a few minutes of steady bidding, I became aware that I was left with just one competitor. I was now determined to continue, come what may. By now the offer price had moved far beyond what I would normally consider paying for single bottle, regardless of rarity, and Andrew was looking across at me with increasing alarm on his face, especially as the other bidder - sitting somewhere on the opposite side of the room, I thought - was showing no evidence of hesitation. However, I do not remember that I ever considered yielding, such was my burning ambition to acquire the wine.

By now the auctioneer was merely turning his head alternately from one side of the room to the other, catching the slightest movement of intent from each of us in turn, and a complete silence had fallen. Finally, his gaze paused away from me for what seemed an eternity.

The hammer fell.

I will not disclose what I ended up paying for that bottle. Even now, I confess to feeling rather embarrassed about it, and a few *sotto voce* expressions of surprise were certainly audible around the room before the auction resumed.

Shortly afterwards, I indicated silently to Andrew that I was ready to leave and we crept out of the cellar and were escorted back upstairs. Bank transfer details and delivery arrangements were taken in the hall.

We drove in silence for a few moments.

"I can't believe you did that" he said finally.

"Nor can I. But look, neither of us is ever going to see a bottle like that again. I couldn't let it go and regret it for the rest of my life."

"I suppose so. I just hope you can afford it."

"Big bonus at the end of the month. That will cover it easily."

"Ah, yes. Well, I expect you'll be looking to sell it on anyway. I mean, it's impossible to tell what is actually left in the bottle with a wine that old."

"Do you know Andrew, I rather thought I'd treat myself to opening it. I've always wanted to join the élite who have tasted pre-phylloxera, and I've got a good feeling about this bottle."

Whether my inner convictions were as confident as my assertions to Andrew, I am now not entirely sure.

I think I will be brief about the conclusion to the affair, as I do not care to dwell on it these days. Suffice it to say that a week or so after my purchases from the auction had been delivered, I had one of the worst days of my life. A scandal about alleged insider dealing had broken that morning at the bank and in the ensuing chaos, trading was temporarily suspended. For a time there was a very real possibility that the firm might fold completely. There was certainly no hope of the expected bonus payments, either for me or anyone else.

I arrived home late, in such a stressed and preoccupied state that at first I did not realise the front door of my apartment had been discreetly forced. As I entered the hallway I could not immediately see any evidence of a burglary. Then I noticed that the small, early Roy Lichtenstein which I had inherited from my father was missing from its place on the wall next to the coat stand.

I walked through the house in dismay. In the living room it was the same story. There was no mess or disorder, but a number of the more valuable pictures which had come with the Lichtenstein were also missing. The thieves were clearly professional and had known exactly what they were after.

I swore inwardly, at length, although I don't recall being particularly upset at that point. Not being much of an art lover, I had only really held on to the pictures by way of an investment and they were all very adequately insured.

Before ringing the police, I went into the kitchen to get myself a much-needed drink, and saw to my intense irritation that the thieves had coolly helped themselves to champagne and food from my fridge. It was then that an appalling thought occurred to me. All my cases of fine wine were at that time stored elsewhere by a private cellaring service, but I had left my precious magnum of ancient Haut Brion in my study, simply so that I could gloat over it for a while.

I rushed frantically into the room. The scene that greeted me remains burned forever on my memory. The magnum was still standing on my desk, but the cork had been removed. Alongside it were my favourite antique brass corkscrew and two of my best crystal goblets, each half-filled with pale amber wine. Lying on the desk was a scrap of paper with a roughly scribbled note:

"Thanks for the hospitality, but this bottle is well past its prime. Hope it wasn't expensive."

Then my eye fell on the cork lying nearby and I saw an ominous dry crack running down its length. I suddenly realised what a fool I had been. Whatever the wine might have tasted like in its heyday, my fabulous magnum of Haut Brion now contained nothing but worthless vinegar.

ODYSSEY

The light is wonderful this morning, intense and silvery. It reflects from the sea of cloud below and burnishes the sky arching overhead. There is a sense of limitless space up here: a vast expanse of emptiness, stretching out to the distant curve of horizon and upwards into the deep blue of the zenith. Even there the space does not end but reaches still further into the limitless, unseen darkness beyond.

Peace and tranquillity prevail in this bright, clear air. It is a place far removed from the frenzied activity of the earth's surface, hidden beneath the cloud. And there is solitude, too, if you are up here alone. A solitude which is tinged this year with sorrow and sad memories. It is the first time he has made the journey on his own, and long-distance flying can be a lonely business when you have no companion.

The weather has been the same for some time now, the dense stratus of cloud forcing him to fly higher than usual and obscuring the familiar landmarks on the ground, the rivers and mountain ridges that mark the long route south. But many years of experience have given him a confident sense of direction and it is safer up here than down in the mist. Besides, the sun is warm on his back and he can continue for several hours yet before thinking of stopping for the night. Perhaps the clouds will have dispersed by then, in time for the evening descent.

His thoughts stray back to the cold, crisp air of the Northern Land. The place of summer, with its wide expanses of tundra, its endless rolling forests and icy lakes. A beautiful and unspoiled country, but too cold in winter. It was there that she died last spring, not long after they had returned, quietly but unexpectedly in her sleep. He misses her so, with an aching sadness that seems unbearable. After so many years flying together as silent but trusting companions, the unaccustomed solitude of this journey brings back his grief.

At long last, there is a break in the cloud below. Just a dark rent at first, but with larger gaps beckoning ahead. The landscape beneath is dappled with shadows. It is time to lose some height and check his bearings on the ground. And there, sure enough, is a familiar streak of glistening water, clearly visible now through the dispersing mist. It is the Golden Sea, etched by the wakes of ships trading with the Orient. Here he can safely cross, at the narrow neck which connects it with the Great Ocean of the south. It is only a short distance over water and then he will be able to hug the coastline of the ocean as it curves round southwards. He knows of some who still use the far western route, crossing by the Pillars of Hercules, but in his opinion this is a dangerous way, especially for any who cannot, or will not, fly high enough. And the weather there can often be bad, too. There are deaths every year, tales of those who did not make it across.

He gains some height again before traversing the neck of the Golden Sea, hurrying on above the water to reach the safety of the far shore. A large skein of geese crosses his path a few hundred feet below, heading determinedly eastwards with military precision. He watches as the leader drops away from the front of the formation to rest, his place quickly taken from behind. Their discipline is impressive and there is undoubtedly safety in numbers, but group flying is not for him. If he cannot be with a trusted companion, he will fly alone. So be it; you cannot alter fate.

He is tiring now and it is time to put down for the night. He has already travelled far enough down the coast to be almost sure of completing the journey in daylight tomorrow. This time of year the days are longer further south, although they do not compare with those of the summertime in the Northern Land, the land of the midnight sun, his homeland.

★ ★ ★

Early morning, the best time. There is a beautiful sunrise this morning. The sun's golden disc edges up from behind the curve of the eastern horizon, painting the surrounding sky with iridescent colour. To the west, he can see the retreating line of the night's darkness. The edge of the dawn is chasing it around the globe, awakening the world in its path. Today there is not a cloud in the sky, although a line of haze is already forming above the horizon. Below lie the folds of a browner and altogether more scrubby landscape, the world of the south, the place for winter.

It has not been an easy night. Landing was difficult, on a stretch of water that was really too narrow and short for comfort and dangerously overgrown at the end. And everyone down there seemed so foreign, somehow distant and inaccessible. Not surprising, really. After all, he must have appeared just as strange to them. Sleep had not come easily and he had spent most of the night worrying about getting airborne safely again. His uneasy dreams were finally broken by the cacophony of a dawn chorus, a reliable and reassuring sound anywhere in the world, although this morning the voices had a harsh and alien quality. In the event, taking off had been easier than he had feared, despite an unwanted encounter with a pocket of low-lying mist. Many years ago there was a narrow escape with power lines hidden in mist, a moment of terror which has lived with him ever since.

★ ★ ★

Now, as the morning wears on, his mood lifts a little,

cheered by the increasing warmth of the air and an anticipation of arrival. Soon the coastline sweeps around to his right, marking the southernmost extent of the Great Ocean. The green finger of the Long Delta appears, standing out in contrast to the brown, arid landscape around it. He remembers a wonderful night they spent together one year down in the delta, its lushness tempting them for a while to stay on and not bother travelling any further south. But thinking of this brings deep sadness back again, memories of their long summers together in the Northern Land, companions in the remoteness of that vast and beautiful place. He is grieving for her yet more intensely and there is nothing that can be done about it, except to wait for time to dull the pain.

There is another memory, too, triggered by the appearance of the Southern Desert, its seemingly endless expanse of featureless sand dunes now coming into view below him. It is not just the heat and lack of water that makes this one of the most dangerous parts of the journey, it is the risk of sand storms. They both nearly perished here a few years ago, when an enormous storm over the desert forced them to fly higher than ever before and then battered them with a screaming gale of blown sand. By some miracle, they managed to stay together and made it across. But only just, and with shattered nerves.

After several anxious hours, just as faith begins to falter, the sand dunes finally come to an end and desert gradually gives way to a greener landscape of scrub and trees. There is always relief at this moment, when the mere hope of a safe arrival becomes reality. This is a time to relax a little and enjoy the surroundings, to fly lower again and slacken the pace. There is now a humid warmth to the air, damp from the recent monsoons. The land below is a beautiful reddish colour, the wide open spaces dotted with herds of exotic animals: elephants, giraffe and buffalo, each kicking up plumes of dust as they move across the dry earth.

And then, at last, the Emerald Lake comes into view. Journey's end. Today it is deep blue in colour, only tinged slightly with green at the very edges. But whatever its hue, the lake is always a heart-stopping sight; a huge expanse of water, stretching to the horizon and glinting in the relentless sun. Towards the near bank, there is a flock of flamingos, not much more than a blur of pink colour from this height.

He starts his final descent, relishing the end of his long and arduous exertion. Further across the lake's surface and almost down now, he sees others from the Northern Land who have arrived before him, already gathering amongst the reed banks along the Home Shore.

The final landing is sweet and easy, as ever. The calm water is warm and rich, the moment precious. There are old friends to greet and a hunger to assuage, but first it is time to fold his aching wings and rest. The long journey south is safely over for another year. The wheel of life has turned another infinitesimal degree in its cosmic cycle and left him unscathed. For now, it is enough just to be alive and to sleep in peace.

THE CIRCUS

The narrow country lane was familiar from distant memory, but Andrew still nearly missed the turn, set back as it was beneath tall beech trees. Stone gateposts flanked the entrance to a driveway curving between high yew hedges, gloomy in the steady rain and strewn with heaps of fallen leaves. When the house finally came into view, he felt a long-forgotten, sickening lurch and began to wish they had not come after all. Three cars were already parked on a wide expanse of gravel beneath the façade of Victorian casements and steeply-pointed eaves. The Jaguar he recognised as Debrett's; the other two vehicles presumably belonged to the surveyor and the valuer from the auction rooms.

"We needn't have come, you know." Susan broke their silence, as if reading his thoughts. "Debrett said he could arrange everything himself, if necessary. The will was quite straightforward."

Andrew did not reply. The rain abruptly turned into a downpour, drumming heavily on the car roof.

"We'll have to wait" he said eventually, raising his voice above the noise of the downpour. "We'd get soaked just getting to the porch."

The house was only just visible through the cascades of water on the car windscreen. Its gloomy bulk seemed to be speaking, screaming almost, but the sound was not heard by anyone except himself.

"We'd better go in" Andrew said, when the rain finally began to ease off. "They must have been there some time now".

The hallway was in darkness, but light streamed through an open side door. Debrett's lean, elegant form beamed at them as he looked up from the papers he was arranging on a heavy dining table.

"Ah, Mr and Mrs Hill, welcome. I take it you found the place again without any trouble," he said. "I'm just getting a few things sorted out for you to sign."

Muffled footsteps and voices from the room above distracted him.

"That will be the estate agent and surveyor, they're giving the place a good going over," he said, looking up at the ceiling.

"I had no idea the house was still fully furnished," Susan said. "All the pictures and ornaments too".

"Oh yes, the old lady wouldn't let anyone touch a thing after Mr Hill died and she moved into the nursing home. An agent from the saleroom is busy doing the inventory as we speak. Of course," he said following her gaze around the room, "as of this moment, everything is still legally yours, so if anything takes your fancy, we only have to let him know."

"I doubt that'll be necessary," Andrew grunted, turning back out of the room.

A darkened corridor beckoned him with disturbing memory. At the end, he pushed open the door into a large living room, shapes of solid furniture suggested by white drapes in the half light.

A cheerful, rather stout man with a clipboard extended a hand in greeting. "Hello, Sir, you must be Mr Hill. I'm Ian Perkins, from the Mile End Auction Rooms. You want everything to go, I understand. I had been thinking of a clearance sale, but there's some nice pieces here, and I'm not sure that doing it in separate lots wouldn't be best."

Andrew smiled, trying to show an interest he did not feel. "I'm leaving all the arrangements to Mr Debrett, but really, whatever you think."

The man bustled cheerfully out. "I'd best be getting on then, I've a few more rooms to do yet."

A silence descended on the living room and Andrew turned towards the fireplace. Large armchairs stood on either side, covered by their dust sheets. His grandmother had always sat on the right during those interminable early winter evenings, her face smiling, needles clicking, not knowing how to talk to a young boy, not knowing what to say or how to amuse. But his grandfather, with his musty smell and wrinkled, blotchy hands, had been different. His grandfather knew what to do. The only way to avoid sitting on his knee had been to plead that he wanted to go to bed early and to bury himself upstairs, hiding under the covers in his bedroom for fear of the darkness.

Andrew went back out into the dimly-lit corridor, the sound of heavy rain beating against the outside window. It had always seemed to be raining during the weeks he had spent here as a child. He had hated the rain, because it had meant he could not escape the house and play in the garden. Turning now up a small flight of steps he saw, with a slight shudder of recognition, the door to what had been his grandfather's study. He paused for a moment, but could not bring himself to open it. The trouble had always been when his grandmother went out to the shops. And on that particular afternoon, because the rain had fallen relentlessly, he had been trapped in the house. He did not have a clear picture of the study in his mind, he just remembered an overwhelming sense of revulsion. And fear. Fear that there was no one else in that great house except himself and his grandfather. He did remember running in terror from the study, running to escape and hide, but where did he go?

Approaching voices brought him back to the present, aware of a cold sweat on his brow. A tall man holding a tape measure appeared down the darkened corridor, quickly followed by a more imposing figure in an expensive suit with an authoritative air.

"I take it you are the vendor Sir? Allow me to introduce myself, Jenkins, from Peabody and Son, and this is Mr Jones, who is doing the survey for us."

"Pleased to see you," said Andrew, meaning it, suddenly. "I hope you've not found anything too much amiss. Structurally, I mean?"

"Oh no sir, it's all in fine order. Roof space dry, not a sign of rot. They don't build them like this any more. I'll be sending my recommendations to Mr Debrett, as instructed, but you can reckon on at least five hundred thousand. I doubt much trouble with the sale, either, there being no chain."

"Well that's good news, anyway," Andrew said. "To tell you the truth I'll be pleased to get it all off my hands."

"Liquidising the assets, Sir, that's the way. Well, seeing as we've just about done up here, we'd best be going now." The two men turned and descended the steps out of sight, leaving him alone once more.

But where had he fled to? He could not be sure. The blind panic of that childhood moment stuck in his mind, but at first the rest was just a blank. Then something half-remembered drove him on, climbing the stairs to the second floor of the house. The rooms up there had never been used, even when he had stayed there as a child that terrible summer. Was it somewhere up here that he had hidden? He had a sudden recollection of crouching in terror behind a door somewhere, tightly screwing his fists into his eyes to shut out the darkness, listening to his grandfather's calls around the house, desperately praying that he would not come up the stairs and find him.

Then, as he stood on the darkened landing, Andrew remembered the circus. It had been the last happy time before the accident, the last time with his mother and father, just before he had been brought here, to this house. In the huge circus top there had been noise and excitement, the smell of sawdust, sweat and animals. There had been a performing elephant, daring trapeze artists and many other exotic delights. Sitting between his father and mother, dangling his feet from the wooden bench, he had wriggled with joy, laughing and clapping in amazement and feeling secure in a way that he never had since.

And then there had been the clown. He had loved the clown best, with his tiny bowler hat, enormous shoes, baggy trousers and stripy, buttoned braces. Suddenly, the memory of his hiding place that dreadful afternoon in the house became clearer. It had been the vivid, happy images of the circus show that he had willed into his consciousness while he had crouched, shaking with terror and distress. Using that precious memory, he had finally blotted out the dark, empty room and the sound of his grandfather's calls.

Andrew stooped down now, in front of one of the row of closed doors before him. With sudden certainty, he recognised the long, ugly crack that ran across the lower part of that door. The shape of the crack was burned into his mind, inextricably linked with the terror of the moment. This was the room, no doubt at all. Sweating again and aware of the pounding of his own heart beat, Andrew hesitated for a moment. Then, with sudden determination he pushed open the door and stepped into the room.

It was almost completely in darkness, the dust and floorboards dimly lit by the bare, diamond-leaded window. He peered into in the gloom for a moment, trying not to believe what his eyes saw but his reason denied. Then he turned abruptly, slammed the door and ran to reach the stairs, taking them recklessly, two at a time.

Back down in the hall, lamplight still shone out of the dining room where he had left Susan and Debrett.

"There you are," Susan said brightly. "We were starting to wonder where you had got to." She held something up. "Do look. I've found this wonderful silver candle chime, just like the ones we used to have when we were little. I'm sure the children would love to see it working. We could bring it out as a treat this Christmas."

Andrew swallowed hard, catching his breath, trying to appear composed as he reached out to take the chime from his wife. It was a striking thing, she was right. Above the four candle holders, silver horses dangled from a circular fan, ready to gallop around the ring once the candles were lit. The circus, again. He felt another sickening lurch, an unwanted recollection of what he had just seen, or might have seen, in that room upstairs only a few moments ago. He almost turned to go back up the stairs and confront reality, but embarrassment in front of the others and the threat of rising panic stopped him.

★ ★ ★

Ten minutes later, still barely able to maintain a semblance of composure, Andrew edged their car back down the narrow driveway, the documents all signed, the business concluded. For a brief second, he allowed his mind to go back to the upstairs room and his panic attack. Surely in reality, the room must have been empty, despite the unimaginable and unformed terror that had flooded out the instant he opened the door. Perhaps fear had blinded him and he had not really seen – what? An old hat stand in the far corner of the room, yes certainly. But had there really been a clown's costume hanging from it? And would it still have been there if he had dared to go back up and reopen the door, or was it just his childhood memory of the circus, sucking him into an imaginary void, back into his terrible childhood dread?

"I'm glad all that's over," he said out loud. "I don't know about you, Susan, but I never want to see that house again."

And silently, he hoped to himself that it had not, indeed, been a terrible mistake to have come at all, and prayed that his old nightmares would not begin again.

UNDER THE KNIFE

"Give me more exposure, damn you!"

David gingerly pulled the retractor back as far as he dared and said nothing, watching Smiley Riley's shaky hands trying to put the last sutures into the anastamosis. No one else said anything either. The uneasy silence was broken only by a rhythmic hiss from the respirator and the beeping of the cardiac monitor on the anaesthetist's trolley. The morning list had progressed more slowly than ever today, testing patience all round. The last case had already been cancelled and they were still running nearly an hour behind.

Finally, Smiley handed his instruments back to the scrub nurse and laid a swab on the oozing graft.

"I think I'm going to ask you to finish off, *Mister* Green," he said, laying a mocking emphasis on the title. "Since you're calling yourself a proper surgeon now, you might as well prove your worth".

He turned away from the table and shuffled out of the theatre, his place opposite David quickly taken by the scrub nurse.

"Will you be wanting Vicryl for the closure as usual,

Mr Green?" she asked, her eyes above the mask betraying her misgivings.

"No, not yet", David muttered, almost to himself, as he lifted the swab. "I can't leave things in a state like this. I'll reposition the retractor for you to hold, please, and see what I can do to stop the leaking."

He looked across at the anaesthetist. "Sorry, John, but I'm afraid you're going to have to keep her under for a while longer".

The anaesthetist gave a resigned shrug and turned away to mark up another set of readings on his chart. The situation in theatre this morning was nothing new to anyone present. Nor was the way his boss was treating him, thought David grimly as he worked away to correct the inadequate suturing and reposition the graft. And, yes, it was true that the humiliations had become more public and spiteful since he had passed his fellowship the previous month. Not to mention the repeated attempts to block his applications for study leave to attend conferences and workshops. Resentment was definitely becoming hard to keep at bay. In fact, recently it had only been his sense of duty to the patients that had kept him going.

★ ★ ★

The theatre rest room had already emptied of staff taking their lunch breaks when David sank down on one of the side benches just over an hour later. He pulled off his mask and cap and reached out for the sandwich he had ordered that morning, by now the last one remaining on the table. Cheese and pickle, with just enough time to eat it before changing and heading back to the ward. Except that before he had managed even to remove the wrapping, the rest room telephone rang.

"Mr Green? It's Julian here. I was wondering whether you could come up a bit before the start of the round this afternoon? It's just that there are a couple of new patients I'm rather concerned about and I'd really appreciate it if we could talk them through. You know, before Professor Riley gets here?"

"Sorry, Julian. I had meant to go quickly round everyone with you beforehand, but I've been delayed in theatre yet again. Only just finished, would you believe? Listen, I'll be straight over, we've still got nearly twenty minutes to sort you out."

David hung up the telephone, glanced again at his watch and went quickly through the connecting door into the changing rooms. Julian Pendry was one of the nicest and most conscientious SHOs he had known. He still remembered the feeling of panic before a professorial round from his own days as a ward doctor, especially as his registrar at that time had been less than supportive. The cheese and pickle sandwich was clearly a lost cause.

★ ★ ★

Professor Riley certainly cut an imposing figure, sweeping onto the ward in his pinstripe suit at the head of an entourage of nurses, students and junior staff. A pecking order of seniority was closely observed as they progressed around the beds, starting with the post-operative cases. Matron positively billowed with importance at the professor's right elbow, followed by David, then Julian, the duty staff nurse and finally the students, the latter keeping a respectful distance behind. Patients were greeted by the great man himself, after he had read their names on the labels above each bed. They were then either ignored or patronised, as first Matron then Julian summarised each case. As usual, any details or problems of management were immediately delegated with a dismissive wave of the professorial hand. "Yes of course, Mrs Smith, but we'll leave all that for the ward team to sort out."

Then straight on to the next bed. First the cursory greeting, then a hasty pulling round of curtains where healing wounds were to be exposed for scrutiny, followed by a shuffling of feet as the students craned their necks to try and see something useful. It was the same each week; nothing varied. Nobody dared to step out of line or question anything for fear of crushing humiliation, which could as easily come from Matron's lips as from Smiley himself.

Within half an hour the circuit of the ward was complete, the ceremony almost over again. No mishaps this week, thank goodness. But before leaving the foot of the last bed, the professor turned to David with a poisonous grin.

"I feel everyone should know that Mister Green is in the process of applying for employment in some very exalted establishments, isn't that right Mister Green? London, no less. We're obviously, ha ha! not good enough for him here any more."

This was followed by a brief, embarrassed silence.

"Well, seeing as you have the day off tomorrow to dream of your future fame, I'm sure you wouldn't mind taking over my side of our own humble outpatient clinic this afternoon? I've some office work I could better do."

David seethed inwardly as professor and Matron turned to walk away together, down the entrance corridor and through into the sister's office to one side. Office work be damned, he thought. Smiley will be in the Dolphin across the road, quietly knocking them back, probably in the company of the professor of anaesthetics, if he knew anything. It was no secret to most people; they were regularly spotted there by junior hospital staff. David had suspected something like it right from the day of his interview for the post here. You could always tell: the tremulous lower lip, the shaking hands holding his application form, the half empty glass of whisky not quite hidden under the desk...

"I'm sorry, Julian." David turned discreetly to his younger colleague. "I know you still have the new patients to clerk, but I'm afraid this means I'm going to have to ask you to take over the follow-ups in the clinic this afternoon. It's a very full appointments list and there's just no way I'm prepared to cancel any of the new cases, just because Smiley isn't going to be there to see them himself. Our waiting times are a disgrace as it stands."

★ ★ ★

It was dark by the time David had released his stressed-looking house officer back to the ward and finished dictating the notes for the last of the new patients attending the professorial side of the clinic. He was tired and hungry, and already his thoughts were starting to turn towards the challenge of the next day. But there was one more thing he knew he had to do before going home. Leaving the half-lit, empty corridors of the clinic, he made his way back once again to the operating theatre suite.

"Oh Mr Green, I'm so pleased to have caught you."

It was the voice of the theatre sister, coming up behind him as he scrutinised the operating list for the following morning.

"I'm really rather worried about that list," she said. "There's a difficult re-do abdominal aneurysm case on first and somebody said you're not going to be there". She dropped her voice. "I mean I know I shouldn't say this, but do you think it's wise that Professor Riley should be doing it with only Dr Pendry to assist?"

"No, sister, I don't, as it happens. That's why I came here to check the list."

David looked unhappy.

"Look I know this rather puts you on the spot, Sister, but it might help matters if you could assist him yourself. You've got much more experience than poor Julian and it might just make the difference. I'm sorry, but you see tomorrow is very important to me. It's a job interview for a very good consultant post and I know I won't stand much of a chance of getting it, but I really can't bring myself to waste the opportunity. God knows when I'll get another chance like it."

"No, I understand. You must go." The sister put a light hand on his shoulder. "You're the most able surgeon we've had here in a long time and you deserve better than this place. I'll do my best tomorrow, of course. But one of these days there's going to be a disaster on table when there's just him about. I fear it, I really do. And now I've said too much already."

"Don't worry, you haven't," David said quietly. "As a matter of fact I completely agree with you. And if anything serious does go wrong, it won't be your fault, you know."

The sister took her hand away and turned to go back into her office.

"Thank you, Mr Green," she said as she turned away. "That's cold comfort of course, but better than none. Anyway, good luck tomorrow, you deserve it."

David said nothing as the door shut behind her. His loyalties were torn, but he had his career to think of. And just for once that was going to come first.

★ ★ ★

"That was the last patient, Mr Green." The clinic staff nurse put her head round the door, clearly anxious to be away. "Will you be needing me any more?"

David looked up at the clock. It was already almost two o'clock.

"No, you go off" he said. "I'm sorry to have kept you so late. I went as quickly as I could, but we were desperately overbooked again. Not your fault, I know."

It had been a long morning clinic and in truth, David had been finding it difficult to concentrate most of the time. The events of the previous day were still too vivid and unsettling. The long journey south, with frozen, snow-clad landscapes slowly yielding to softer, greener scenery as the train rattled its way across the harsh border country, down past the industrial north and on through the Midlands. By the time they were approaching London, it had seemed like a different world entirely, almost as if winter had never been. But the excitement of arriving in the capital had changed to apprehension as his taxi deposited him in bright sunshine, outside the gleaming new hospital buildings.

There had been five other shortlisted candidates, two of them internal, all highly qualified and seemingly brimming with confidence as they chatted in the waiting room. Being last on the interview list had not helped his nerves. But when he had finally been called in, the interview panel had been welcoming, even sometimes encouraging, and he had come out in better spirits, knowing he had given a good account of himself. Later, of course, a predictable despondency had set in during the endless trek back up north. The numbing effects of travel were compounded by fatigue and the winter darkness, slowly shutting out the view from the carriage window.

★ ★ ★

It was snowing again now. He could see heavy flakes falling outside the high window of the examination room. And the phone had not rung all through the long morning in clinic. The chairman of the interview panel had promised to let him know their decision by telephone today and trying not to think about the expected call was becoming increasingly difficult. Not that he really thought he would be offered the post, but at least knowing the worst would put him out of his misery.

In the event, he had just finished his last dictation and was about to go and try and catch the canteen when the telephone finally did ring. His heart missed a beat.

"Mr Green?"

False alarm. It was an internal call, the familiar voice of the ward staff nurse.

"I'm so glad to have caught you. I'm really very worried about the aneurysm re-do from yesterday and I don't know who else to call. It's Dr Pendry's afternoon off and no one seems to know where Professor Riley has gone, but I do think someone needs to have a look at the patient as soon as possible"

"I'll be right up, Staff," David said into the telephone. "Five minutes."

"I bet I know where Smiley is," he murmured to himself as he scooped his stethoscope off the clinic desk and headed out of the door. "But that's not going to help now."

The curtains were drawn around the bed when he got to the ward and the briefest of examinations confirmed his worst fears.

"I'm sure the graft is leaking, Staff. We'll need to get him back to theatre as soon as possible. If I could leave you to sort out a porter, I'll try and drum up an anaesthetist and get a team together up there."

★ ★ ★

Five hours later, David slumped down in a sagging easy chair, overcome by the mixture of exhaustion and relief which he had come to associate with successful closure after difficult surgery. The patient was now in intensive care and out of his immediate hands, but alive and with a chance, at least. The theatre rest room was deserted and dimly lit at this hour, its windows dark and the detritus of the day not yet cleared by the night cleaners.

"Oh, it's you Mr Green, I thought you'd be gone by now." The theatre sister paused in the open doorway, bag and coat in hand. "You look all in and I'm not surprised. Don't you think you should go and get some rest now? I gather the patient's stable again thanks to you."

"Well, he's off the table, at least," David said. "Although whether he'll make it through the night is another matter."

"Well if he doesn't, the blame won't lie with you, Mr Green. I know I shouldn't say, but you know my views on the matter. Incidentally, how did it go yesterday? Any luck?"

"Probably not, judging by the fact that I still haven't heard," David replied.

"You'll be sure and let me know what happens, won't you, though?" The sister pulled on her coat and turned to go. "I'm going off now. It's just the on-call staff left if you need them, but I'd go and get some shuteye, if I were you."

The door closed behind her and David kicked off his bloodstained theatre clogs, trying to decide whether to make a cup of coffee here, make a final check on the ward or simply have done with it and go straight back to his hospital lodgings. Maybe, he thought, something should be done about Smiley. Maybe someone should be told. After all, there was the issue of professional accountability, not to mention a certain responsibility for members of the medical profession to look out for each other. He looked across at the telephone on the wall and wondered.

Just then, it rang.

★ ★ ★

The link corridor was in darkness. At the far end, the main swing doors leading into the ward were closed. But to one side, light streamed out from an oval window in the door of the ward sister's office. David stopped quietly in the dim corridor and peered in. The scene was no great surprise. Smiley and Matron sat either side of her desk, glasses and a bottle of whisky between them, engrossed in conversation. Suddenly, David felt something snap inside him. Giving little thought to the consequences, he pushed open the door noisily and confronted them.

"Mr Green, what a surprise. Working late?" Smiley's expression was gently mocking, his speech more than a little slurred.

Matron looked uncomfortable, but kept silent.

"Yes, as a matter of fact, I am," David said. "I've just finished patching up that aneurysm case of yours from yesterday, since no one seemed to be able to get hold of you."

For a moment it was Smiley's turn to look uncomfortable. Then he rallied and rose to his feet in a threatening manner.

"Now look here, Mr Green, you can't just come blundering in here like this, interrupting a private discussion..."

"No, you look here, Professor Riley!" David said, fighting back the temptation to let his pent-up anger get the better of him. "I've just about had enough of being treated like this and I think you should know that my long-standing concerns about your professional competence, not to mention this" - he gestured at the bottle and glasses on the table - "have finally come to a head. I should also tell you that I've sought advice and informed the appropriate authorities."

Smiley's face puckered with rage and he gave an angry bellow.

"What the devil do you think..."

"I've just had a long conversation with some very helpful people at the General Medical Council," David continued, his voice remaining level and controlled, "with the result that you should expect a very thorough investigation into your practice at this hospital within the next few days."

Smiley crumpled back into his chair, his right hand shaking. Matron looked at the floor, her hands clenched on the desk and white knuckled. There was a moment's silence in the room.

"And one more thing you need to know," David continued, "I've just been offered the post in London and I have accepted it. The offer is unconditional and I won't be needing your references any longer. They want me to start as soon as possible and I'll be handing in my notice formally tomorrow morning. Meanwhile, I bid you both goodnight."

Without waiting for a response, he turned and strode back out of the office and down the darkened corridor. There was no remorse. He was sure that he had done the right thing. Now it was time to start looking forward.

MR ALBERT

"Alouette, come back!"

Taking no notice, the hen scurried down the gravel path towards a door in the far wall of the vegetable garden. It was a small, grey and very determined bird.

"Stop! Stop at once! You're being a very naughty lady!" Arms flailing, Emily ran as fast as she could, but just before she could reach out and grab the bird, it slipped under the rotten wood at the base of the door and vanished from sight.

"Oh Alouette! How could you?" Breathless and flushed, Emily stamped her foot in frustration. The old rusty lock suggested a door that was not likely to open easily. At first she hammered hard on the woodwork with her fists, but then she calmed down a little and stopped to think. Perhaps it would be worth just trying the door handle.

A firm twist of the iron ring produced a loud click, as if there was a latch on the other side. Emily pushed hard and to her surprise the door yielded, creaking reluctantly on its hinges.

She stopped in her tracks, framed in the open

doorway. Before her lay an old orchard, its rows of wizened apple trees stretching down a slope away from the walled garden. There was an atmosphere of long neglect and a sweet smell of rotting fruit. Heaps of windfalls lay in the long, damp grass, alongside dead and broken branches from the trees.

"What this orchard needs is a good pig" declared Emily, her voice barely carrying in the stillness. Then she spotted the grey hen, pecking at a rotten apple under the nearest tree. Without hesitating, she darted across and grabbed it.

"Got you, naughty lady, and this time I'm not letting you go!"

She held the bird close in her arms, keeping the wings tightly against its body so it could not hurt itself. The hen clucked and wriggled before conceding defeat, going limp and making crooning noises. Silence fell again.

Just then, a rhythmic clacking started to echo from further down the orchard slope. It was the unmistakeable sound of an axe chopping wood. Still holding the hen firmly in the crook of her arm, Emily decided to go down and investigate. She trod carefully as she went, avoiding the rotting fruit beneath her feet.

"Hello there."

Emily started, nearly letting go of the hen. She turned quickly towards the voice.

"Don't worry, I'm very friendly. I don't get many visitors here."

The man was elderly, with grey hair, a drooping moustache and a stained linen shirt open at the collar. A patched and worn tweed jacket hung from a nearby branch. He put his axe down next to a pile of chopped wood and extended a calloused hand out to her in a curiously formal gesture. Emily backed away slightly, uncertain.

"I'm Albert" the man said, smiling at her suddenly. "What's your name?" His eyes were at the same time both kindly and a little bit sad, Emily thought.

"I'm Emily," she said at length, "and this is Alouette." She tightened her hold on the hen in her arms. The bird clucked and crowed quietly, as if aware it was being talked about. There was an uneasy pause. Emily felt that she should explain things a little further.

"I've come back from India to go to school and until term starts I've got to stay here with Grandma," she ventured at last. "She lives on her own. And it's not much fun with no one to play with. Nanny doesn't count, so I've only got the hens and they're always getting out and running off."

"Ah, you must be young Mr Lionel's girl," the man said.

"He's not Lionel," Emily pouted a little. "He's called Papa, except when Mama speaks to him, when they think they're alone."

"And what's he called then?" the man asked, smiling again.

"Darling. I think it's soppy, don't you?"

"Oh well I suppose if you're madly in love..." The man stopped and looked sad again.

Emily decided a change of subject was needed.

"What are you doing?" she asked, settling the hen again as it tried to slip out from her grasp.

"Well, I'm collecting all the dead wood and cutting it up." He paused, looking around him, shaking his head slightly. "And after that, there's all the windfalls to gather up and the grass to be cut."

"Why?" Emily said. "I mean why do you have to do it?"

"Someone's got to," the man said. "The place has been left untended for far too long, in my opinion."

This seemed a very reasonable reply, but somehow it didn't invite further enquiry. Emily was just considering what to say next when the sound of a distant handbell broke the silence.

"That means tea time," she said. "I'll have to go now. Can I come and see you again?"

"Well... that depends." The man looked at her uneasily, twisting his hands together. "But it would have to be our secret. Don't you go telling anyone else now, will you?"

"Of course not," Emily said dismissively, turning to go. "I can keep a secret, you know. Come on Alouette, it's time you got back to the coop."

"Goodbye!" the man called out to her receding figure.

Emily turned back at the doorway in the wall.

"Bye, Mister Albert."

Then she pulled the door closed behind her with a free arm and was gone.

★ ★ ★

"Nanny, is this Alouette's egg?" Emily looked doubtfully at the egg cup on the breakfast table in front of her.

"Well now, why would such a thing matter?" Nanny bustled.

"Because she's my favourite hen and her eggs are always more speckley than this one." Emily's teaspoon was poised.

"And if I were to say that it came from one of the other hens, would you still eat it?" Nanny replied, turning her back and climbing onto a footstool in front of the linen cupboard. Emily considered the problem for a moment and decided in favour of eating eggy soldiers. Her teaspoon made a satisfying crunch as it dug into the top of the egg.

"Why can't I go out today, Nanny?"

"How many times do I have to tell you not to talk with your mouth full?" Nanny turned to the table and began putting the used porridge things onto a tray. Emily swallowed the last of her soldiers and looked at Nanny with her special stare.

"I don't think it's fair if you won't tell me."

Nanny put the tray back down on the table and looked towards the window.

"In the first place it's raining, and in the second there are things going on this morning that are no business of yours."

"What things?" Emily persisted.

"Ask no questions and you'll be told no lies. And another thing while I'm at it, your grandmother has told me that the old orchard is to be out of bounds in the future and the door kept locked."

"That's because I went in there yesterday to rescue Alouette, isn't it?" Emily could not help looking slightly crestfallen. "But what if she gets out again?"

"Then you're to come and tell me. There's been people going in there who shouldn't be, so it's no place for a young girl like yourself. There now, I've said too much already." Nanny stacked the rest of the breakfast dishes, picked up the tray and made towards the scullery door.

"But he's only looking after the..." Emily's voice trailed off and she bit her lip. A secret was a secret, after all.

Nanny paused in front of the door for a moment, then turned to give her a piercing look. Emily squirmed in her chair and decided that, on this occasion, keeping quiet was probably the best policy.

"I've no idea what you mean by that, young lady, but you mind what you've been told and stay away from the place in future," Nanny said at last. "And you can make use of a wet day to get out your exercise books. It'll stand you in good stead when your new school starts next week."

Emily waited until the door had closed behind her and tripped quickly across to the bay window, scrambling up onto the window seat to look out. Rain was pouring down. Leaning over to get a sideways view, she could just see the kitchen garden down below, its high brick wall completely hiding the orchard beyond. As she looked down, a tall man in a brown raincoat came into view, followed by two uniformed policemen, one holding the lead of a large dog. They walked briskly away from the house, crossed the gravel paths of the kitchen garden and disappeared from sight through the old door in the wall.

Emily knelt at the window transfixed. Because of the dog, she worried for a moment about a hen escaping from the coop again. Then she felt a horrible guilty feeling growing inside her. All this had something to do with Mister Albert, she felt sure. She had kept their secret, of course. But there was something wrong about the whole affair, something she didn't understand. Perhaps she shouldn't have told Nanny about Alouette's escape and the discovery of the orchard. Perhaps she had said too much.

Emily remained at the window for a long time, staring out at the rain and the garden wall below. But no one came back through the door.

★ ★ ★

"It's so good to see you again, dear. There aren't many

people who stop by to see an old lady like myself, these days."

Nanny put the tray down on a small table and busied herself for a moment, setting out the cups and pouring tea.

"It's a pleasure, Nanny. It wasn't far off my route anyway" Emily said. "And I'm pleased to see you keeping so well. Have you been settling in all right?"

"Well, I mustn't grumble. The lady from the council said I was lucky to get anything at all on the ground floor. But it's not the same as having your own place, even if they do bring a hot meal round every day. It comes in tin foil, ready heated, you know. All I have to do is have a plate ready. Anyway, there you are dear, freshly brewed."

Emily balanced the tea cup and saucer on her knees, there being no other obvious surface available.

"What about the neighbours, though? I heard loud television coming from up the stairwell when I arrived. I hope they don't keep you awake."

"Oh no, dear, I'm far too deaf these days for things like that to worry me. It's the man that lives across the road that's the trouble. He keeps hens, you see, and they're forever getting out, making a mess all over the path at the front here. Do you remember the hens at your grandmother's? You know, that summer before you went off to school. You used to be keen on those hens, gave them names and things. Do have a biscuit."

Emily took a biscuit from the plate next to the

teapot. Chocolate digestives, bought specially for the occasion, she thought.

"I remember the hens very well, Nanny. There was one who kept getting out and running off. She got into the old orchard once and I chased her and found a strange man in there. Albert, I think his name was."

"Oh yes, caused a bit of a stir, that did. I'd forgotten that." Nanny looked rather distant and fell silent.

"So what was all the fuss about, Nanny? I never found out, you know."

"Well, I don't see there's any harm in saying now. It was all a long time ago." Nanny peered at Emily through her half-moons. "And you're a grown up lady now, after all." She paused for a moment and fiddled with a teaspoon. "His wife was your grandmother's housekeeper, you see. Before we got there, that is. What I heard was, a bit before we arrived some silver stuff went missing. Of course the housekeeper denied it and everything, but your grandmother was so sure it was her that had taken it she had her dismissed, even though it was never proved she'd done it."

"And the husband?" Emily was all ears, the story having aroused a childish curiosity.

"Well, he worked there as the gardener and odd-job man. Loved the place, apparently. And, well, I don't like to speak ill of the dead, but your grandmother could be a bit spiteful when she wanted. When nothing came of the accusations, she made them both leave at the same time."

"So when I let slip to her about finding a man in the orchard..."

"She wasn't best pleased. Called the police and everything."

"Yes, I remember seeing that from the nursery window. But, Nanny, did you ever hear what became of them?"

"Him, I don't know. But she... well, I might as well say. She did herself in. It was in the papers a while after you went off to school. Couldn't stand the shame of it all, they said. And then, of course, I left soon after myself. Nothing more for me to do there, what with your parents coming back at Christmas and everything."

* * *

Later, Emily drove back out to the London road musing on the childhood memories awakened by her visit. The image of the man in the orchard stuck particularly in her mind. His sad expression and quaint manner were as vivid as if it had all happened only yesterday.

"Poor Mister Albert," she said out loud, waiting for the traffic lights to change.

INHERITANCE

The view from the head of the valley was picture perfect; an idyll of beautiful and remote countryside, secluded and cut off from the outside world. A narrow lane led down through beech copses and grazing sheep to Pinbury House, nearly half a mile distant. The house was a curious affair, part Strawberry Hill Gothic, part Palladian, with a glass cupola mounted in the centre of its roof, glinting now in the strong summer sunshine. The intricate, manicured gardens were separated abruptly from the surrounding meadowland by a low, encircling ha-ha. It was as if the whole ensemble had been set down like a child's toy in the middle of native countryside.

William paused to admire the peace and isolation of the place, something he often did on his visits home. Then, after a few minutes' quiet thought, he climbed back into his car. He had been driving with the hood down and the seats were sticky with the heat, the steering wheel uncomfortable to hold. He restarted the engine and edged slowly across a cattle grid before picking up speed down the access lane.

The main façade of the house was still and quiet in the hot sunshine, the windows on the upper floors flung wide open and the front door left ajar. William parked his car on the broad gravel sweep at the front of the house. He climbed the steps, pushed open the door and walked silently into the lofty hall behind.

It was cool inside, with dim light filtering down onto the marble floor from the central stairwell. Opposite him, double doors were flung back to give a view into the room behind the hall and through to the garden beyond. The sound of voices and laughter led him out to the cloistered terrace at the rear of the house. A group of girls were engaged in a noisy and chaotic game of croquet on the back lawn. Two were his young twin cousins; the others he did not recognise.

"William, how lovely to see you, have you been here long?"

His Aunt Mary got up from her chair just outside the French windows and advanced towards him, proffering a cheek for a kiss.

"I've only just this minute arrived", William said. "I thought the place was deserted at first."

"Oh, we're all outside in this weather. The children are loving it, as you can see. But how are you? You must be exhausted after such a long hot drive. Come and sit down and have a cool drink."

She led the way to a table and chairs set out on the terrace and poured two glasses of lemonade from a large jug covered with beaded muslin. Shrieks and more laughter came from the lawn.

"We're down for the weekend. To lend support, you know," she said. "I let Vicky and Liz bring some school friends along as well. I thought they'd be more easily kept amused that way."

William sat watching the children for a moment, envying their happiness.

"The twins have grown since I saw them last", he said. "How old are they now?"

"We had their tenth birthday party last week" his aunt replied, "just before the news about your poor father. I was so sorry to hear he had taken a turn for the worse."

Will looked uncomfortable. "I got your letter yesterday" he said after a brief silence. "I'm pleased you wrote, Aunty, don't take me wrong, but all the same I still don't see why my mother couldn't have contacted me herself. She always seems to leave things to you when there's any kind of crisis."

"You mustn't be too hard on your mother, Will, she's been through a lot recently, you know." His aunt did not meet his eye as she spoke.

"But you're too soft with her" William said. "And she's always using you. I expect she just turned to the bottle again this time, as usual. Anyway, where is she now? There's something I need to have out with her."

"Oh darling, you will take care, won't you? Actually, I haven't seen her all afternoon, nor your uncle Leonard, either. Although I seem to remember him saying something about going for a walk."

"And Hen," William said "is she here too?"

"Inside, I think. She said she had a headache at lunch."

More shouts and laughter from the lawn, the children tumbling in a writhing heap on the grass, all pretence of playing a proper game abandoned. How wonderful it would be to regain that innocence, William thought. Not to know of the suffering and wrongs that life had in store.

"Well, if mother's not around, I'm going in to see father" he said, getting up and walking back towards the French windows.

"Will..." his aunt called after him. "Will, don't expect too much will you..." Her voice tailed off as he vanished inside.

★ ★ ★

The library was cavernous and gloomy, and was lined by bookcases from floor to ceiling except for two ornamental alcoves and a monumental carved stone fireplace. The room had the musty smell and melancholy atmosphere of a place that is seldom used. Henrietta sat on the window seat to try and catch enough light to read by. It had always been her favourite place in the house, somewhere to retreat from other people and be alone. She was fond of her twin sisters, but no longer felt young enough to join in with their high spirited outdoor games.

Besides, something was wrong today. Normally, visits to Pinbury were looked forward to eagerly, but this time there was definitely a bad atmosphere. Henrietta had formed the distinct impression that her mother and aunt had somehow fallen out with each other.

She turned to look out of the window at the garden in late afternoon sunshine. The children had gone indoors and the croquet set was now cleared away. Just then her father appeared through an archway in the topiary hedge at the far side of the lawn, immediately followed by her aunt. Henrietta watched as they walked together across the grass and out of sight around the side of the house.

Then the door to the library clicked open and William walked in, smiling.

"Well if it isn't my favourite cousin," William said. "I thought I might find you in here. Do you mind if I join you for a bit?"

"Will, how wonderful!" She leaped up and ran across the room to give him an affectionate hug. "You've no idea how pleased I am to see you. Everybody's been driving me potty this afternoon."

"Well I'll try not to do likewise, but I can't promise" William said.

"Of course I didn't mean you. You're different, silly. Come and sit next to me by the window."

She dragged him over to her seat, but not before glancing anxiously into his face.

"There's something wrong, I can tell", she said, as

they sat down together. "You've just been to see your father, haven't you? Poor you, was it just too awful?"

"It was pretty grim actually," William said quietly, looking down at the floor. "All the twitching and jerking has got so bad. But the worst, you know, is that his mind's gone now. He didn't even know who I was this time. And his eyes are empty. They're just blank - there's no person left behind them."

Henrietta put an arm around his hunched body. "Oh Will, I'm really so very sorry. I don't know what to say."

"You don't have to say anything. Just having you here is a comfort." He gave her hand a squeeze, then hesitated for a moment. "Hen, it isn't only about poor father's own suffering. There's something else. It's rather awful, actually."

Henrietta turned to look at him with an anxious look on her face.

"I know I can tell you, Hen, you've always been such a friend to me," William said. A silence followed. "You see," he continued after a while, "I went to talk to the college doctor yesterday, after I got Aunt Mary's letter. I told him everything about father and explained that I was worried because I thought I was developing twitching in my hands. He examined me and said that it was just stress. But then he told me that the thing my father has is hereditary and that actually there is a high likelihood of it being passed on to me, though it's still too early to be sure one way or the other. I think he just assumed I already knew, but of course I didn't, really. I've only just started to suspect it. And that's what makes it all so much worse. That no one ever told me before, I mean. Mother must have known. Surely, the doctors must have told her years ago."

Henrietta felt William's body go stiff and saw him fighting back tears.

"Hen, the truth is, I'm frightened," William said at last. "And angry. I'm also very angry."

Henrietta held her arm more tightly around his shoulders, unsure how to respond.

"Will, I promise you I had no idea," she said finally. "My parents never said anything about it, really, honestly. It's all just so ghastly. What are you going to do?"

"Apparently there is a test that would show whether or not I have inherited the disease, but the college doctor advised me not to have it. Not to insist on knowing. Better to make the most of the present and live in hope, that kind of thing. He said he'd seen people where the test had come back positive and they'd let it wreck the healthy years that were left to them, or even topped themselves."

Henrietta suddenly withdrew her arm and stared at him, appalled.

"Will, that's awful. You mustn't think of such horrible things. Oh, damn. No, I'm sorry. It's easy for me to talk. That was a stupid thing for me to say." She reached out and took his hand again. "But there must be a chance that you might not have inherited this horrible thing after all, surely you have to hang on to that?"

William stood up abruptly, his face white and tense, and stared for a moment back at his cousin.

"Hen none of this is your fault, and you've been a brick to hear me out. But I'm not sure even you can help me any more. I don't know whether I'll be able to face the future. I don't even know whether I've even got a future to face." He turned and started to walk towards the door. "But I do know exactly what I'm going to do right now," he said, not looking back, "I'm going to find my mother."

★ ★ ★

All the ground floor rooms were uncannily quiet, but the sound of distant voices drew William down the dimly-lit service corridor at the back of the house to the scullery, where he found an agency nurse deep in conversation with Ellen, the housekeeper.

"She's in the orangery, Master William, she sent for a drinks tray not half an hour ago," Ellen said in reply to his enquiry.

Retracing his steps for a short distance, William turned down a short connecting passageway and opened the door into the orangery. This was an airy space, backed by a high brick wall, its high glass ceiling largely obscured by a jungle of exotic trees and dangling creepers. Hundreds of potted cacti covered a bench set against the long row of side windows, overlooking the vegetable garden. Early evening sunlight streamed in through the glass. Areas of the stone floor were still damp from recent watering and the atmosphere was hot and humid.

"Will, darling, they told me you were here. Come and have a drink and tell me all about college. I'm dying to hear what you've been up to."

His mother was sitting in a wicker chair next to a table bearing a tray of bottles and glasses. William couldn't help noticing that her voice was already thickened by drink. Probably not the first of the day, he thought.

"Mother, I'm sorry, but I'm in no mood for drinking. I need to have a serious talk with you. Now."

"Why, whatever's the matter? And do sit down, you're making me nervous standing over me like that."

William remained standing, staring unblinkingly at his mother. He spoke in as controlled a fashion as he could muster.

"I need to know why you have never told me the truth about father's condition, about how it runs in the family and is likely to affect me, too."

His mother blanched visibly and set her glass down on the arm of the chair.

"Oh Will, who have you been talking to? You mustn't believe everything you hear, it's simply not true...."

"What do you mean it's not true?" Will cut in. "As a matter of fact, I've been speaking to the college doctor and the truth is now quite clear to me. In the first place, I will very likely develop poor Father's illness before I'm very much older, and secondly you must have known that all along and haven't had the guts to tell me. And thirdly, I am not a child any longer and I shouldn't have had to find it out in this way."

He stared down at his mother, anger barely controlled, white knuckles clenching the back of an empty chair.

"But Will, you don't understand, really you don't, things are not as simple as that. We..." she stopped momentarily, looking down into her glass "... I was going to explain everything, but the time was never right. And now it all seems just so complicated..."

"Complicated!" William was shouting now, unable to contain himself any longer. "I have no idea what you mean by that, but I don't think it's complicated. I only think that you really don't care about me at all any longer. Have you any idea what I'm going through now?"

His mother put down her glass and got to her feet. "No, Will! I can't take this, it's all too much, what with poor Arthur the way he is and now you shouting at me like this, I just can't take it!"

She fled, wailing, back through the connecting door into the house.

"I hate you!" William shouted after her, sweeping her glass from the arm of the chair so it smashed onto the floor, releasing a powerful smell of gin.

There was a brief silence.

"I say, steady on."

William swung round. His Uncle Leonard was

standing in front of the rows of cacti, the glass door from the garden open behind him.

"How long have you been here?" William demanded angrily. "Do you make a habit of snooping on other people's conversations?"

"Now that's unfair," his uncle protested. "The way you were shouting anyone could hear you, even out in the garden."

He came up to William and reached out to try and put an arm around him.

"I know this a difficult time for you, old chap, but you'll have to go easy on your mother, she's going through a lot at the moment."

"*She's* going through a lot - what about me!" William cried, shrugging off his uncle's arm and walking away. "Does anyone ever consider me?"

He pulled open the door to the house and glared back at his uncle. "Do you have any idea of the position I've been left in?" he shouted. "Does anyone even care?"

He slammed the orangery door behind him and started to run back up the passage, tears streaming down his face.

* * *

The town was like something out of a fairy tale - a Gothic fantasy, Henrietta thought, although the illusion was somewhat shattered by the hordes of tourists thronging the streets. She looked up at the stone gatehouse in front of her, checked the name of the college on her street map and slipped quickly through into the comparative peace of the courtyard beyond. A bowler-hatted porter was sitting behind the window to one side of the entrance, but he appeared engrossed in a newspaper and did not notice her. A group of boisterous undergraduates with tennis rackets clattered into the quadrangle.

She asked for William by name and was directed through one of the ivy-clad archways, up the stone staircase beyond and then to a door on the first-floor landing. To her relief, the door was clearly marked with his name. She set down her heavy bag and knocked.

"Come" a voice barked from within, "it's open."

William and another young man, both in academic gowns, were poring over books at a large desk in the centre of the room.

"Hen! What are you doing here?" Her cousin leapt up from the table.

"Oh, I'm sorry, I thought you'd be alone," Henrietta said, suddenly losing confidence.

"What a lovely surprise!" William said, pulling her into the room by one hand. "Here, come right in. This is Geoffrey, a friend of mine; Geoff, this is Henrietta, my cousin."

"Very pleased to meet you. Let me help you with your bag", the other man said, advancing with a smile, hand outstretched. "Don't worry about me, I was about to go. We were just finishing anyway, weren't we, Will?"

After polite protestations on all sides, Geoffrey left the room, closing the door firmly behind him. Once they were alone, William came up to her, face beaming. He seized both her hands and peered anxiously into her face.

"Hen, what's happened? I mean it's wonderful to see you, but why are you here? And you don't look well. Actually, I think you'd better sit down right now, before you fall down."

He swept a heap of periodicals from a large old divan and beat dust off with his hands. "I'll make some coffee in a moment but first you must tell me everything."

"Oh Will, I'm really sorry to crash in on you like this, but I had to come. Something dreadful has happened and you had to know and... it's silly, but now I'm here at last and I don't even know where to begin..."

"At the beginning?" Will suggested gently. "It's usually best."

"Well, it's Mummy and Daddy", Henrietta said. She paused, swallowing hard. "They've left each other. They've been arguing and shouting behind doors for weeks and then it all came to a head last weekend. Mummy's taken off with the twins to go and stay with great Aunt Clara and last night I had a dreadful row with Daddy and... it's all just so dreadful." She stopped speaking again for a moment, looking down at the ground. "In the end, I made Daddy tell me everything. It turns out he's been... unfaithful to Mummy for years and years, even since before they were married. And it's still going on and she's never suspected until now and... I'm sorry, Will, but in the end I just said I couldn't stay at home any longer and I couldn't think of anywhere else to go..."

She tailed off as William sat down beside her. He reached out both arms to give her a big hug, silently holding her close.

"Poor Hen. And I thought I had all the problems" he said at last.

"But that's not the only reason why I'm here," Henrietta cried in agitation, pulling herself away from him. "I had to come to see you straight away, because something else has come out of all this. Something important. Something good for you, Will."

"I don't follow," William said, "what do you mean?"

"I mean," Henrietta lowered her voice again, almost whispering. "I now know that you are not going to inherit Uncle Arthur's illness. You don't even have to have the test. You're going to be fine, Will."

"How can you possibly say that?" William withdrew his arm suddenly and looked at her in amazement.

"Because, Will," Henrietta reached out and clasped both his hands in her own, "because Uncle Arthur isn't your real father. You are my half brother."

THE DARKEST HOUR

The inner vestry door led down a flight of stone steps, through the unused choir stalls and on into the looming void of the church. On an early winter's evening, the cavernous interior space was only partly lit; a pool of light around the far end of the nave near the west door and another above the altar at the other end of the building. In between the building was in near darkness, but as usual, it was warm. The vicar had always insisted on keeping the building heated in winter, and also leaving it unlocked until seven o'clock on weekday evenings, so that parishioners and passers-by could drop in for private prayer and meditation. In all James' three years as a curate there, no one had ever been seen to take advantage of this, except perhaps for occasional homeless waifs and strays seeking comfort before their cold, outdoor nights. St Ursula's was in a poor neighbourhood, a semi-derelict area in the eastern part of the city and even the main Sunday morning service attracted only a thin turnout of the remaining faithful these days.

The elderly lady with all the bulging carrier bags was

there tonight, sitting as she often did right at the far end of the nave near the main door. James had long since given up trying to approach her; she always fled, silently clutching her carrier bags, back out into the street. Where she slept he did not know, although her face was regularly to be found amongst those at the parish Friday soup kitchen, where since time immemorial it had been the duty of the curate to give the lunchtime homily. There was no such thing as a free lunch, James thought grimly, not even for the homeless.

He turned to the east end of the church and knelt down in one of the empty front pews, contemplating the plain wooden crucifix on the altar and the dark, rather dirty leaded window behind. He tried, for the second time that day, to calm his thoughts and pray, but as before, found that he could not.

As he closed his eyes, the images of the simple, white-painted room in the hospice and his late wife's sad eyes came flooding back again, making his appeals to the Almighty seem futile and worthless. She had been so brave and calm during those last days, refusing drugs so she could try and stay alert with him. He had spent countless silent vigils at her bedside in that quiet, simple place, her pale hand placed loosely in his and her trusting look fixed on the crucifix hanging at the end of the bed. He had sometimes knelt beside her bed to try and pray, silently in the way that she had always done herself.

And it was then, before she died, that he had first realised that his faith had left him.

When the doctor had first told them the bad news as they sat holding hands together in the consulting room, he had known that the time ahead would be a challenge to his beliefs. But he had not been prepared for the speed with which anguish and bitterness would overtake him, nor for the emptiness which followed in its wake. It had been a cruel blow. With his second curacy almost at an end and the challenges that St Ursula's had brought, both his career as a priest and their lives together giving service to God had all seemed to be just over the threshold. And now - nothing. Just darkness and despair.

The sound of wings high above his head broke into this troubled reverie. He opened his eyes and looked up into the dark vaulted space beneath the tower. Another bird must have got in. Several of the small panes of glass in the tower windows had been broken for as long as he could remember, clearly visible from the outside in daylight, along with the crumbling areas of stonework which the Diocese continually protested it could not afford to repair. James got up from his knees and sat in the pew. He turned around and saw that the bag woman had gone, no doubt sensing that it was near the time for the church to be locked. He was quite alone.

For a moment he tried to rationalise his predicament. The news of his first posting as a fully fledged parish priest had come only a week after his wife's funeral. Rather cruel timing he thought. The rector had congratulated him, as had many of the other mentors he had known in his long years of training. But no one suspected the truth. His conscience told him that he should not accept the post, should not embark on a life of deceit, acting out a role, going through the motions, with a soul that was empty of faith. Sitting now in contemplation, he decided that he must confide in someone before it was too late. He would have to grasp the nettle and go to talk openly with the rector. James had always thought him a good man, if somewhat orthodox and limited in his views.

The sound of wing beats drew his eyes upwards into the darkness again. Perhaps he should tell the rector about the bird trapped in the tower, while he was at it.

★ ★ ★

On Saturdays, St Ursula's was left open later into the evening, in case there was a need for a last-minute personal confession before the following morning's Eucharist. There rarely was, it seemed, although just down the road people queued up, James knew, for formal confessions in the Roman way. That tradition had never attracted him, although it meant that the rival establishment would be less achingly empty of human souls on a night such as this.

But not quite empty, James noticed. The bag lady was back again, huddled in her usual place. He turned to the altar, genuflecting and moving slowly up the steps to check that everything was in place for the next day's morning service. He walked across to the lectern to open the bible at the first lesson and put in a marker for the second.

Then he stopped, standing for a moment in the warm near-darkness between the transepts, motionless, his eyes turned inwards. He had written a letter earlier that day, explaining to the Bishop why he felt unable to take up his new appointment. He had not posted it. He knew that was a failing of courage on his part, but nevertheless it had suddenly seemed a dauntingly irrevocable step. The consequences would be endless and humiliating, he felt sure. But neither had he torn up the letter, destroying it and all it stood for. And what was that? Did it stand for honesty and courage? Or was it just an admission of failure, his failure as a priest?

The sound of wings again. The poor bird must still be there, unless another had got in. He peered up into the gloom beneath the tower and just for a brief moment, he thought he saw something large and pale move across the void. Surely nothing, it must be his imagination. He was overwrought, and with good reason.

He sat on the end of a pew, feeling the letter weighing heavy in his cassock pocket. There seemed little point in trying yet once more to pray. He knew by now that this would not work. Instead, he went over the afternoon's interview with the rector. There had been no sense of surprise or dismay at James' admissions. All perfectly understandable, he had been told. The rector had seen it many times before, especially in young priests under great personal strain, or experiencing troubles in their personal lives. Not in the least surprising in his particular case, and nothing to worry about. Almost certainly just a natural reaction to the undoubted trauma of his poor wife's terminal illness and to the stress he had been under. And yes, *of course* he should take up his new appointment. He shouldn't even think of resigning! His work as a vicar in charge of his first parish would soon distract him and his true faith would surely soon come flooding back. Even if it didn't, at least at first, the rector had personally known several priests who had carried on regardless, providing pastoral care and support to countless souls in need. Moreover, James had been assured, his particular posting was known to be reserved for young priests showing great promise: it had been a stepping stone to many a glittering career in the Church. And the rector had personally heard James' name being mentioned in this regard around the corridors of Diocesan power.

Overall, James felt it had not been either a terribly helpful or encouraging interview. In fact, he had written the letter immediately afterwards, with the full intention of posting it straight away.

He looked at his watch: it was time to lock up, even for a Saturday. The bag woman had already left.

He walked down through the darkness of the central aisle to the west doors and slid their bolts across with an echoing thud. Turning back up towards the chancel, his eye was caught by something lying on the tiled floor beneath the gloomy void inside the tower. How strange. He had not remembered seeing anything there a few moments earlier. Coming closer, he saw that it was a large and beautiful feather. Far too big for a pigeon, surely, and anyway, quite the wrong colour, all cream and gold.

He peered up into the tower again but saw only darkness. Bending down to pick the feather up, he was struck by its unexpected lightness. As he held it in his fingers, the oddest sensation flooded through his body. Like the rush from a first morning cup of coffee, but infinitely more powerful. His thoughts reeled for a moment and then, suddenly, with an absolute conviction that astonished him, he knew clearly what he must do. Still holding the feather, he strode quickly out through the vestry, turning off lights and locking the doors as he went, and walked out into the clear, cold air of the night outside.

★ ★ ★

"And now to the Father, Son and Holy Ghost..."

James reached the end of his inaugural sermon in his first very own church and stared out yet again in amazement from the pulpit. The building was full of light and packed with people. Partly drawn here by curiosity to see the new vicar, perhaps, but nonetheless an impressive turnout. In fact, the entire service was proving to be a wonderful, uplifting experience. He announced the last hymn and stepped down from the pulpit, basking in the sound of a proper choir and the massed voices of a full and eager congregation. The difference from Sunday morning at St Ursula's was beyond measure in every sense.

In truth, he had known it would be so, even after the few short days since his arrival. Here was a parish bursting with people eager to be involved, almost running itself under the momentum of its own enthusiasm. As the notice board in the church porch testified, there was a rota for almost everything imaginable, with no empty spaces for months to come. Even the rather dowdy lady playing the organ had unexpected depths, James thought as he ascended the altar steps to give the final blessing, which was promptly followed by the sound of a triumphant and expertly-executed Bach toccata.

He turned his head to bask in the sunlight streaming in through the stained-glass east window, a recently-funded commission depicting the archangel Gabriel with golden wings outstretched. And as he looked at this image, he felt a sudden exultation, bordering on ecstasy. His career as a priest lay ahead of him and he could barely wait to embrace it.

Back in the vestry, James dismissed the server with the customary blessing and found himself, for the first time that day, alone. He turned to the wooden desk where he had laid the feather on his treasured family bible immediately before the service. But the feather had gone. Somehow, he had known that it would no longer be there. With just the same certainty that he knew his faith had returned, and that it would never desert him again.

DOLPHINS

The dolphins were there again, fleeting silhouettes arching against the sunlit swell. They looked as though they were playing like children, but it was more likely that shoals of fish were bringing them so far in to feed.

Luke put down his coffee mug and gazed out of the window, watching them frolic in the bay below. The morning had not been productive - only a few hundred words, which should probably be erased anyway - and it was a welcome relief to rest his eyes away from the computer screen in front of him. Perhaps he should call it a day and go out into the spring sunshine. Long experience had taught him that if words did not flow early on, things would only get worse if he tried to persevere into the afternoon.

As he got up from the desk to stretch his legs, his eye fell on the parcel delivered earlier by the irrepressibly cheerful local postman. It would be advanced copies of *The Dragon's Lair*, as promised by his publishers before he had left London. By way of encouragement, he pulled open the wrapping and removed one of the brightly-covered hardbacks stacked inside. The dust cover was illustrated in a garish and surreal fashion, similar to the preceding volumes in the series. Not the style he would have chosen, but he had been repeatedly assured it helped sales, and anyway he didn't get much say in the matter.

As a matter of fact, fantasy fiction had never been Luke's goal as a writer, but he seemed to have a certain talent for magical landscapes and mythical beasts, and this had at least helped to pay the bills for the last few years. It was yet another attempt at a more serious vein of writing which had brought him out here to the cottage once again, with the intention of getting away from the interruptions and distractions of the city. An attempt which currently lay stalled by writer's block on his word processor. Never mind, tomorrow was another day. Maybe a walk would clear his thoughts and feed the muse.

Stuffing a half-eaten chocolate bar and an apple into a pocket, Luke picked up his ivory-headed stick, slammed the back door behind him and walked across the narrow stretch of rough scrubland that separated the cottage from the cliff top path. The light today was of an intense, luminous kind only found on sea coasts, and it forced him to screw up his eyes for a moment while they adjusted from the dim interior and his computer screen.

He stood for a moment looking out into the bay. The dolphins had gone, but the view was magnificent, uplifting. To the west, high cliffs stretched around a broad headland topped by gorse-strewn pasture and a maze of dry-stone walls. The other side of the bay was bounded by a narrow and vertiginous promontory, with sheer sides which culminated in an isolated rock pinnacle known locally as the Bodkin. On an impulse, Luke determined to climb down to the beach which was hidden under the cliffs immediately in front of the cottage.

The way down was familiar from his previous visits, but steep and rocky and still requiring care in the descent. As he negotiated some rough steps down a tight zigzag bend, his left knee gave a sudden warning, a reminder of the old injury which made him glad of his stick. Then, just before the beach came into view, the sound of shouting made Luke pause. That was annoying. The place was remote from the nearest village, being reachable only along several miles of country lane, and could normally be relied upon as a place of solitude. Apparently not today.

Sure enough, round another bend in the path, he looked down to see several children chasing after a ball on the expanse of sand below, their excited cries echoing off the cliffs. He considered turning back, but then remembered the tiny secluded inlet hidden on the other side of the Bodkin. The tide was out far enough to walk around from the main beach, and he judged that there would be several hours before it came back in again. He finished clambering down, strode quickly across the beach away from the ball game and on to the flat rocks beneath the cliffs surrounding the promontory.

Bright sunlight reflected off rock pools under his feet. The shouts of the children were soon replaced by a screeching tumult from seagulls disturbed from the rock ledges above his head. He clambered through the gloomy cleft between the tip of the promontory and the towering rock of the Bodkin, emerging at the top of a narrow sea inlet with a rough pebble beach at the far end. Here at last he could count on some solitude. Reaching the pebbles, Luke picked his way over them to the surrounding cliff, wincing occasionally when an uneven step caught his knee, until he could finally make himself comfortable sitting with his back against a slab of rock. He took out the apple and ate it thoughtfully, gazing out at the strip of horizon visible between the Bodkin and the cliffs opposite. Way out to sea, a huge container ship moved slowly across the bay before disappearing behind the cliffs. Few small boats came out this way; fishermen from the village usually avoided it because of treacherous rocks submerged beneath the cliffs. The sun was warm. Luke dozed.

* * *

He was awakened by the rhythmic, harsh grating sound of undertow, the sea waves pulling back from the pebbles at his feet. It was clear at once: he had slept too long and the incoming tide had trapped him while he slept. A deep swell was lapping at the cliffs either side of the inlet and the base of the Bodkin was entirely submerged by heaving water, breaking into foam against the rocks. A raft of cloud had covered much of the sky and the late afternoon light was already beginning to fade. Luke stood and shivered in the chill air, fighting back panic. There was no route up the cliffs; he had looked down from the top of the promontory often enough to be sure of this, and also to know that at high tide the sea entirely filled the inlet, leaving no refuge. He was not a strong swimmer, but the only means of escape was to brave the sea and make his way back around the pinnacle.

Time was of the essence. Trying not to think of possible consequences, Luke pulled off his shoes, decided that he could not risk trying to take either these or his stick, and waded unsteadily down through the shallow breaking crests into the heaving sea.

The water was cold, colder than he had imagined, and as he launched himself off the stony bottom he discovered how hard it was to make headway against the incoming tide. But with an effort of will, kicking hard with his legs and riding the nauseating motion of the swell, he gradually drew abreast of the rocks around the bottom of the Bodkin. The narrow channel between these and the mainland cliffs was filled by rough and treacherous-looking water, and he judged that it would be safer to try to swim out around the seaward side.

Despite increasing pain in his left knee he kicked out further, conscious of the danger of being swept in against the steep rock sides of the pinnacle. Eventually, to his relief, the cliffs behind the main beach came into view, just visible each time the swell of the tide carried him up to a crest.

It was then that he realised he was no longer making any headway landward; despite his best efforts, the cliffs seemed to be further away each time he caught a glimpse of them. He had not expected this current, and it was undoubtedly drawing him out to sea. To make matters worse, his whole body was now becoming numb with cold and he was starting to shiver uncontrollably.

Luke did not usually scare easily, but he was frightened now, appalled at the deep water beneath him and the thought of drowning, of the terrible moment when water flooded into the lungs, the last breath expelled and swamped by death. He kicked out desperately, fighting against cramp in his frozen legs.

As he did so, something large and smooth brushed against his side under the water. Uttering an involuntary cry of alarm, he thrashed against it, desperately trying to move away, images of all sorts of sea monsters flashing across his mind. Then a sleek black body with a rounded fin broke the surface a few metres away, followed by several more in quick succession, riding the swell all around him. The dolphins!

One of them nudged gently up against him under the water again, as if trying to push him towards the shore, whilst the face and snout of another reared up immediately in front, its eyes large and unblinking. It occurred to Luke that he might even try reaching out and clutching at one of the creature's fins, but at that moment there was a shout from further away behind the undulating walls of sea swell, distinctly a woman's voice.

"Hold on, I'm coming!"

As if on a prearranged signal, the dolphins vanished as quickly as they had come, just as her head appeared over the next crest of water rolling towards him. She looked very young but was swimming quickly and competently towards him.

"Hold on there and I'll help you back in" she called again. "The current is quite dangerous out here."

"Oh thank you!" Luke gasped, almost taking in a mouthful of seawater. "Stupid of me. Got caught by the tide. No strength".

Strong hands caught hold of his head on either side and held it up above the water.

"Don't talk", she said "just roll over onto your back and let me take your weight. Don't worry, I won't let you go under."

She was behind him now, cradling his head beneath the ears and pulling him backwards over the undulating crests and troughs of water towards the beach. A sudden shaft of golden light appeared across the water, almost blinding him, and he saw the sun appear briefly in the strip of clear sky between cloud and horizon before it sank out of sight. When they reached the other side of the breaking foamy water near the shore, her strong arms gently pushed him upright and he realised that he could now just feel the sand and gravel of the bottom.

"I have to go," she shouted above the noise of the breakers. "You'll be fine now".

Exhausted, Luke staggered up through the heaving shallows and out onto the narrow strip of remaining beach, his feet smarting from sharp stones and shells in the sand. He was cold, spent and without shoes, but he was safe: he was not going to drown.

Catching his breath as he reached the water's edge, he realised that the woman was no longer with him. He turned to scan the sea beyond the line of breaking waves, but she had completely disappeared. This, even in the relief and emotion of the moment, did not entirely surprise him. She had been an exceptionally strong swimmer, despite having used both arms to support his head above water. And he was sure that he had not imagined the fish-like thrusts of her powerful body and its scaly touch in the water below him as she had pulled him to safety.

But the dolphins had known, long before he did.

THE JEWELLED EGG

The street was in an old and neglected part of the city which, as yet, had escaped the march of contempory urban development. A labyrinth of alleyways, still surfaced with their original cobbles, was hemmed in by overhanging timbered buildings which jostled together at crazy angles, in places almost blocking out the sky. Old-fashioned street lamps hung over the cobbles, attached by wrought-iron brackets to the house walls. Most of the ground floor windows were bowed outwards with thick old glass panes. Above some of the doors, faded letters announced businesses long since vanished. Quaint and picturesque it undoubtedly was, but there was also a sad air of dereliction about the place.

Rounding a bend in the street, Alex stopped and looked up at an old shop sign consisting of three gilded spheres hanging from a rusty bracket. The sign was immediately familiar and brought back times past from his childhood. It had been around these quiet old alleys that he had often walked with his father, during the weekends when he had been allowed to visit. He knew they had come down this particular street more than once, because the pawnbroker's shop had fascinated him as a child. His father had explained the meaning of the sign and he still had a clear memory of standing on tiptoe to look in through the murky shop window underneath the hanging globes, entranced by the clutter of objects left out on show.

Alex walked up to the window and peered through one of the thick glass panes. The interior was in darkness with no sign of life, but the heaps of dusty artefacts were still there and there was something about the appearance of the shop which suggested that it was still operating as a business. His father's apartment, the one he had taken after the separation, must have been quite close by, but Alex didn't feel like looking for it again now. As a boy, he had enjoyed the weekends spent with his father, if only because it had made such a contrast to the stifling formality and affluence of his stepmother's house. He had always felt intimidated there, even before his father had moved out, when they had still been living together.

He had never known his own mother, although his father had often talked to him about her when he grew older. All he really knew was that she had died in some sort of accident shortly after his birth. His earliest proper memories were of living with his father and stepmother in the big, lavishly-furnished town house which had always been in her family. Although mostly away at boarding school, he had never been happy in that house, especially after his father and stepmother had fallen out, during those awful summer holiday weeks of raised voices, slammed doors and embarrassed, silent mealtimes.

Alex turned from the shop window and started to walk back down the narrow alleyway, wanting to shut out the past again. The winter evening was already drawing in and he was getting cold. He had come further than he had meant to this Sunday afternoon, and it would take some time to find his way back to his bedsit and the mean comfort of the electric fire. There were enough shilling pieces to keep it going for a while, but money, as ever these days, was a problem. To make matters worse, the restaurant where he did a late shift washing up had informed him last week that his services were no longer required, so he was yet again without a source of income. He had at least been warm and adequately fed at his stepmother's house, even after his poor father had succumbed to leukaemia and the weekend visits had ceased.

Until, that is, he had returned one day after dropping out of college to find that a maid had discovered the syringes and needles in his bedroom. It hadn't taken much of an excuse for his stepmother to throw him out, he thought bitterly. But right now he was penniless, without even the money to pay next week's rent, and something had to be done.

As his steps turned into busier, more familiar streets with the clamour of people and traffic, he resolved that he would try and talk to his stepmother again. It would be the first time in two years and maybe she had mellowed towards him in that time. Surely, with all that wealth, she could not refuse him help in his current predicament. He would go boldly back and appeal to her, and he would do it tomorrow.

* * *

"You'd best wait in here", the maid said, opening the door to a large reception room. "She's not come down yet this morning, but I'll go and tell her that you're here."

She vanished up the staircase. Alex walked into the large, opulent room and looked around at the expensive furnishings, pictures and ornaments that filled it. His memory of the room was vague, but then he had rarely been allowed into the best rooms, as his stepmother had called them, even when he had grown beyond childhood.

Pausing to look out of the window back into the street, he reflected that the day's enterprise had not been encouraging so far. Walking up the road between the exclusive Georgian terraces and their private street gardens, he had experienced an unexpected trepidation. In fact, he had nearly turned back when he had reached the building that had once been his own home, at least in name. Confronted by the formality of the stone steps and huge shiny black door, all once so familiar, his courage had almost failed him. But nevertheless he had tugged on the bell pull, hearing again the familiar sound of the door chimes as they echoed down the hall inside. The maid who finally answered the door had been quite unfamiliar - something he should have anticipated, he supposed - and had shown great reluctance even to let him in, despite his attempts to identify himself. In fact, the whole affair was rapidly becoming very humiliating indeed.

The sound of voices outside the room brought him suddenly back to the present. He turned as his stepmother entered the room, his hands shaking slightly.

The interview, for that is what it was, did not go well. She was obviously not at all pleased to see him and was at pains to make it clear that she had a busy morning in view and that he was not part of it. She could not imagine why he had come back here, but if it was money he was after, the answer was no. She was most certainly not going to finance his drug taking, nor was there any use in his denying it. And finally, if he had not got the gumption to take gainful employment, that was his lookout and she no longer considered herself responsible for supporting him.

"I will send the maid in with some coffee, and then I'm afraid I must ask you to leave" she said. "My bridge party will be coming in half an hour and I can't have you still here when they arrive."

She swept out of the room, calling the maid as she did so. Alex had barely managed to get a word in edgeways before she was gone, not even giving him time to realise his own feelings.

Suddenly a great anger welled up inside him, and he began to feel an overpowering sense of injustice. This arrogant snob of a stepmother had failed *him*, not the other way around. This was a woman who should have been a mother to him, loved and cared for him through childhood and into adult life, but instead she had held him at arm's length for the best part of twenty years. She had not even attended his father's funeral.

He glanced again around the room. It was filled with all the pampered trappings of wealth, and yet all she could spare him was a cup of coffee. On a bitter impulse, barely aware of his own action, he reached for an expensive-looking ornament from one of the display shelves and slipped it into his pocket. He was damned if he was going to go away empty handed, and she could certainly afford to do without it. Without pausing to consider the consequences, he stalked angrily out of the room, brushing past the maid with her coffee tray, crossed the hall, pulled open the front door, clattered down the steps into the street and strode off, not looking back.

★ ★ ★

There was a light on in the pawn shop, streaming out of the window onto the cobbles in the early evening gloom. It was the only light visible in that part of the street; the outside lamps had not yet come on and the windows of all the surrounding buildings were dark and sightless, speaking of abandonment. Alex's mood rose slightly. It looked as though the shop might be open today, so perhaps his plan was not doomed to failure after all. And something definitely needed to done, without delay. That morning, two rather threatening men in dark suits had called on him.

"Mr Stevens?" (more rhetorical than enquiring, Alex had felt.) "We're here on behalf of your mother's insurance company..."

"Stepmother."

"I beg your pardon sir?"

"I said stepmother. She's not my mother, she is only my stepmother."

"Well, if you say so sir, but that makes no difference to us. There's a certain item gone missing from the house and before a claim is paid out, you understand, a few enquiries have to be made. For example, we understand that you paid your mother... beg your pardon, stepmother... a visit the day the item was reported missing. Now, would you have anything to say about that sir?"

No, he did not have anything to say, nor, to his surprise, did he lose his nerve. The two men eventually left, but they made it clear as they did so that the matter was not, in their opinion, closed and that he could expect further visits, possibly from the police. At first Alex had panicked, thinking only of how to rid himself quickly of the pilfered object hidden amongst his dirty underwear. But he needed money, and the item was surely worth a bob or two. Then he had remembered the pawn shop and what his father had told him about how it worked. Surely this would be the perfect way get rid of the stolen ornament and make himself some cash at the same time.

A cyclist clattering past on the cobbles - no lights, crazy fool - brought Alex's attention back to the present. He crossed over to the shop window and once again peered inside. Although lit from inside, there was no apparent sign of life. He turned and confronted the shop door, a forbidding gothic affair studded with fake black bolts. Rather surprisingly, it pushed open easily, setting off a jangling bell.

The interior of the shop was dimly lit by a single bare light bulb and had a musty, damp smell. The walls were covered with a multitude of artefacts: various clocks, none of them working, hunting horns, antique bed pans, dark oil paintings in ornate frames. Beneath the glass counter there was a jumbled collection of dusty, lacklustre jewellery, pocket watches and ornaments. On the wall behind the counter there was a faded notice:

"Terms: Strictly six weeks. Twenty per cent will be levied."

After a few minutes a short, rather corpulent elderly figure shambled into the room through a curtained partition.

"Can I help you, young man?"

"Ah, yes, I... I have something I'd like to sell... er... pawn."

Alex pulled the object from his pocket and removed its wrapping of old socks. The old man shot a single sharp glance towards him and arranged a square of greasy leather on the counter. Placed on this, the item in question suddenly looked rather inconsequential to Alex: a gilded ornamental egg, covered in a bright coloured, decorative patterning and mounted on miniature claw feet. But heavy, he'd noticed that. The pawnbroker examined the thing briefly, apparently without much interest, turning it over in his hands and replacing it on the counter.

"I can't offer you much", he said, "I doubt I'd be able to sell it." Then after a brief silence: "Twenty pounds, that's my final offer."

"I'll accept that", Alex said without hesitating, breathing inwardly with relief.

Taking the money and the pawn ticket the man handed across the counter, he turned to leave, but then paused, suddenly uncertain again.

"I suppose I can rely on complete discretion?" he said.

The man looked curiously at him for a moment. "I never ask where things come from, nor why they're here", he said finally. "That's none of my business. Good afternoon."

Alex pushed open the door and left, the door bell jangling again as he pushed the money deeper into his pocket.

★ ★ ★

His jaw throbbed mercilessly, occasionally adding a stabbing pain that brought tears to his eyes. Clutching his face in his right hand, Alex looked around the rather dismal waiting room with its bare lino floor, peeling bench seats and cold strip lighting. There were only two other patients there, both elderly and silent. A rather bored-looking receptionist was absorbed in an obviously personal telephone call whilst painting her finger nails, something she managed to accomplish without dropping the receiver. It had taken quite a while to locate a National Health Service dentist in the area, but he was damned if he was going to spend what little money he had left on teeth. The cash from the pawnbroker had not lasted very long.

Although he had been right to get rid of the stolen ornament, he reflected. Only the following day, two plain-clothes police officers had paid him a visit, brandishing a warrant to search his digs. It had been with some relief that he had felt able to let them search in vain and watch them leave empty handed.

The sound of a dental drill, only too audible through a thin partition wall, brought Alex out into a cold sweat. Seeking distraction, he reached for one of the rather tatty, dog-eared magazines lying in a heap on a small table. It was a back issue of *Country Life;* over two years old, he noticed, scanning the cover. He flipped through pages filled with predictable details of country mansions for sale and articles on horse riding, gardening and hunting.

Then something caught his eye which stopped him dead in his tracks. It was a full-page advertisement for an auction by Bonhams, with colour pictures of some of the more noteworthy items offered for sale. And there in the bottom right-hand corner of the page was a photograph of an ornamental jewelled egg. Not just any old ornamental egg, but surely the same one that had just been causing him so much trouble, distinct in every familiar detail. Disbelievingly, Alex stared first at the picture and then the caption below it.

"Decorative egg in solid gold and precious stones by the Russian master jeweller Fabergé. One of a pair made for Tzar Nicholas 1st around 1898. The current whereabouts of the identical companion piece is not known."

Realisation slowly dawning, Alex looked down at the reserve price in disbelief. Then, toothache forgotten, he leaped to his feet and rushed out of the waiting room into the street, upsetting the magazine table and letting the door bang shut behind him. He ran at full pelt through the traffic and crowded pavements and on into the maze of tiny backstreets beyond.

Perhaps because his thoughts were in such turmoil, he soon found himself hopelessly lost, breathlessly trying one alleyway after another in an increasingly blind panic. Finally, with searing lungs and aching legs, he recognised the little old cobbled street he was seeking. Or thought he did, because rounding the corner to where the pawn shop should have been, he saw only rows of abandoned buildings with boarded windows. He stopped, disorientated and gasping for breath. Then after a brief moment of confusion, he saw the bracket which had once supported the three golden spheres and beneath it the unmistakable mock gothic door. On which was pinned a notice bearing the words: "BUSINESS PREMISES FOR SALE OR LET".

He was too late.

NOW YOU SEE HER

"Well I think it's all a load of crap. If you can't see something, then it's not there. End of statement. This invisibility thing is just a fantasy, fairytale stuff."

Martin put his empty wine glass down amongst the debris on the coffee table and leant back in his armchair, exhaling cigarette smoke with an air of finality.

"Oh come on, Martin, stop being so bloody boring," Jodie said irritably. "How do you know what science may uncover? Christ, people didn't even believe in electricity until Faraday came along, and look what it can conjure out of thin air. Light, magnetic force, lethal shocks..."

"But that's not the real point, is it?" interrupted Simon quietly. "The interest is in the logic, the philosophy behind the concept of visibility. I mean, like the existentialist approach. Is something still there when you stop looking at it?"

"Balls!" retorted Martin.

Simon flushed slightly, looking uncomfortable.

"Shut up, Martin" Jodie looked across at him

angrily. "At least try to be civil. They are our guests, you know."

"Sorry, Simon, no offence meant." Martin looked chastened but sulky.

"Well, at least Malcolm seems to be enjoying his little game with us." Anna broke the rather embarrassed silence. "I know that smile. Come on, Malcolm, you started all this, so it's your turn to get in the firing line. Tell us what you really did see in China."

"I told you" Malcolm said. "I met a sort of mystic, a village elder who could make things disappear and reappear at will. I didn't expect anyone here to believe me and the fact that you lot don't doesn't worry me in the slightest."

He got up from the sofa he had been lounging on and walked over to gaze out of the window with his back to them, hands thrust into his pockets. "God, what a day. The weather's filthy out there," he said, irrelevantly.

"I suppose if you look at it in reverse, as it were," Simon said after a brief pause, "people are quite capable of seeing things that aren't there. Sometimes what they see is so real they can even paint it. I've seen it in exhibitions. The art of the insane. Isn't that right, Anna?"

"If you mean visual hallucinations," Anna said carefully, "I'm not so sure. I mean some psychotic patients do describe such things. I know that from my time doing psychiatry. But it's difficult to know whether they're just imagining what they claim to see, rather than actually seeing it, if you see what I mean."

"Dear Anna, that's wonderful, but just too serious and convoluted." Jodie laughed out loud, reaching out to tap her friend's hand affectionately. "What I want to know, Malcolm, is whether the things this mystic, or whatever he was, made invisible could be touched, like, actually felt by your hands. I mean, were they really still there?"

"Oh, as to touching, I couldn't tell you that" Malcolm said airily, sitting back down on the sofa and starting to roll himself a cigarette. "I was never allowed to get that close. But I can tell you that you could still see people's clothing. It was moving about quite naturally, as if it was still being worn. So I suppose in that sense they were still there."

"What, you're not still trying to make us believe that this chap actually made real people invisible?" Martin looked disbelievingly across the coffee table at their lodger. "Are you sure you weren't high on something yourself at the time, Malcolm?"

"Quite sure." Malcolm retorted calmly. "I never dabble in anything stronger than good quality grass, which you yourself share in occasionally, Martin, and I'm not going to rise to crude insinuation. It is a fact that very real people were made to disappear and they could only be seen by the physical movement of their clothing. I saw it more than once with my own eyes, and I was as sober as a judge." He tapped the end of his joint into the ashtray, leaned backwards and closed his eyes, clearly enormously pleased with himself.

"And they came back?" Simon asked incredulously. "Did they stop being invisible after a period of time? I mean, how long did this charade last? I'm sorry but I really can't swallow it, not without proof."

"You musn't be so sceptical, love." Anna snuggled closer to her boyfriend and leant affectionately on his shoulder. "There are more things in Heaven and Earth, Horatio... It pays to keep an open mind, even in science, you know."

"Hear, hear!" Jodie chimed in. "I'm all for open minds. Speaking of which, given the amount of booze some of us have drunk, would anyone like another brew of coffee? Go on, Martin, it's your turn to get off your arse and act a bit more like a host. Take some of this rubble back into the kitchen and go and make another pot. It's my birthday, after all."

Martin reached forward to pick up two empty wine bottles and got stiffly to his feet. "There's no need to carp at the rest of us, just because you're still virtuously sober" he retorted. "You're capable of getting pissed too, when you want to, you know." He paused. "Actually, I'm not sure there is any coffee left."

"Oh Martin, I told you to buy more yesterday. You're hopeless!" Jodie looked annoyed again.

"OK, OK, *mea culpa*." Martin put up his hands in a mocking gesture. "I'll go out and buy some more now."

"Thanks, Martin" Anna said, languidly kicking off her shoes and lifting her feet onto Simon's lap. "If you're going to brave the elements outside just so we can have more coffee, I think you're a saint. Even if you are a hopeless one."

Martin shot her a conspiratorial grin and went out into the hallway. "I still haven't found my keys though," he called back. "Someone will have to let me in again."

"If you were just a bit more tidy, perhaps you wouldn't keep losing them" Jodie shouted as the front door banged shut.

Silence fell again, broken only by the sound of rain lashing at the window.

"Jodie, I do wish you and Martin would stop sparring so" Malcolm said at last, still leaning back with closed eyes. "You've been at it since first light and it's starting to get on my nerves. Did he forget your birthday or something?"

"Mind your own business, Malcolm," Jodie retorted tersely. "Good lodgers shouldn't eavesdrop, you know."

"Oh come now, my dear, would I do such a thing?" Malcolm's voice had that slightly mocking, patronising tone that only larger-than-life characters seem to be able to get away with. Jodie put her feet up on to the table, saying nothing.

For a while, a sense of inertia set in across the room. The wind howled outside. No one moved or spoke.

"But you never answered my question, Malcolm." Simon said eventually, stretching out his arms and stifling a yawn. "I want to know if you actually saw these invisible people become visible again, rematerialise, so to speak?"

"Oh yes," Malcolm replied, blowing out a perfect smoke ring. "The effect never lasted very long, it was always completely reversible." Suddenly, he leant forwards and fixed his gaze on the three others in the room. "Tell you what, would you like to see a demonstration?"

"Just what do you mean by that?" Simon looked across at him curiously, gently dislodging Anna's feet from his lap.

"Well actually I managed to persuade this chap to part with some of his magic potion," Malcolm replied nonchalantly, getting up from the sofa. "Don't run away, I'll just go and get it." He left the room.

"I'm not sure I'm in the mood for party games," Anna said, once Malcolm had gone.

"Oh, come on, don't be a spoilsport, I think this could be amusing." Jodie smiled across at Anna. "It could be fun to see if even Malcolm can pull this one off with a straight face."

"Well I'm all for a bit of fun," Simon said, "but if he's trying to be serious, I'll take some convincing."

"I heard all that, o ye of little faith," Malcolm said, walking back into the room. He sat down, swept aside the bottles and glasses and placed a small silver-coloured phial on the coffee table with a theatrical flourish. "Now then, who wants to be guinea pig?"

"If you mean to make one of us invisible, then I volunteer" Jodie said, laughing. "I'm the birthday girl and anyway, it might just give Martin enough of a surprise to get him off his high horse when he gets back. Assuming your trick really works, Malcolm." She sat up straight and adopted a pose of playful attention, smoothing down her dress. "So what do I do, then?"

"You drink this" Malcolm replied levelly. He reached out and handed her the phial across the table.

"Look, is this really safe, Malcolm?" Anna said, suddenly anxious. "I mean this is just a trick, right? You're not going to do anything silly, are you?"

"And bite the hand that gives me shelter?" Malcolm looked amused. "Of course it's safe, I saw it done several times without any upset. I simply want to convince you lot that I'm not just spinning a tall story."

Simon looked at him intently. "I am now totally confused by you, Malcolm," he said. "I no longer have any idea whether to take you seriously or just laugh at your tomfoolery."

"You should always take people seriously, Simon," Malcolm replied with mock gravity. "It's impolite not to do so. Now then, prepare to be amazed. Are you ready, Jodie?"

"Just a minute" Simon said reaching over to the table lamp. "It's getting quite dark in here. I take it you have no objection to some light on the scene, Malcolm?"

"Be my guest" Malcolm said waving his hand toward the lamp. "I can assure you that I have nothing to hide."

Simon flicked the switch and a low light illuminated the circle of chairs and sofas around the table.

"Right" said Jodie briskly, "time for the denoument." Holding up the phial, she removed the stopper and playfully waved it towards Simon and Anna. "Sure neither of you want a share of the action?"

"Don't, Jodie." Just for a second, Malcolm's voice betrayed a hint of agitation. "You must take it all yourself."

"Look Jodie, are you sure...?" Anna leant towards her friend and grasped her arm, holding it down for a moment.

"Absolutely. Here goes."

Jodie shrugged off Anna's hand, held up the phial and drank the contents off in one quick draught. There was a brief silence as she put the empty container back down on the table.

"Now then, I hope everyone is watching carefully, she said, with a slightly nervous laugh, "because I'm not sure if I'll be able to tell if anything's happening. Believe it or not, I've had no experience of being made invisible before."

"Well, I can't see anything different" Simon said, peering closely at her. "What did it taste like, by the way?"

"Nothing" Jodie replied, still laughing. "Just like water. All the best potions do, I imagine."

"Give it a moment" Malcolm said tersely. "You may think this is a game, but you wait and see."

Just then Jodie stood up suddenly, putting her hands up to her chest. "I'm suddenly feeling peculiar," she gasped, "everything's going faint..."

"Jodie!" Anna got up and reached towards her. "Are you OK? What's happening, you don't look right!"

By now, Simon was also on his feet. "My God! Something really is happening. Look at her face! It's going... fuzzy. I don't believe it!"

"Anna, I can't feel your hand!" Jodie cried, her voice rising in panic. "I can't see anything properly any more, it's all dissolving... Malcolm, what's going on?"

Malcolm had gone pale, his theatrical manner suddenly vanished. "It shouldn't be like this," he muttered. "I don't understand it."

"Perhaps a glass of water," Anna cried, turning to run to the kitchen. "Perhaps if she tried to drink a glass of water..."

"It's a bit late for that" Simon said, pointing in Jodie's direction. "Look, she's disappearing!"

From where Jodie had been standing there came a faint wail of terror, followed by a sound like exhaled breath. Then silence. The others stood motionless, looking down in horror. There was nothing left to see but Jodie's clothes, lying unoccupied in a crumpled heap on the floor.

"Christ, Malcolm, what have you done?" Simon turned to him accusingly. "This isn't a joke any longer. What the bloody hell are you playing at?"

Malcolm rushed forwards and reached down to the pile of clothes. He picked up the dress with shaking hands. Out fell an expensive pair of skimpy black knickers. He watched frozen in horror as they landed softly on the floor.

"I don't understand it" said Malcolm again. "Something's gone wrong."

"Oh no, please not!" Anna said, holding a hand to her mouth. "Where is she? What have you done to her?"

"Well come on, think, man!" Simon said angrily. "This isn't how you described what you saw in China, is it? You said their clothes moved around as if they were still there and you never mentioned them being terrified. So what the hell do we do now?"

"I don't know" Malcolm said unsteadily. "Maybe if we wait for a bit... I just don't understand what can have gone wrong."

"Well, a return seems a little unlikely now, I'd say" Simon said, picking up Jodie's dress. "Unless she rematerialises in the nude, that is..."

"Malcolm," Anna interrupted suddenly. "You seemed very insistent that Jodie should drink all the contents of that bottle herself, what was that all about?"

"Just something the old man said when he gave me the elixir," Malcolm said cautiously. "He said that it would be very dangerous to allow it to act on more than one person at the same time. He was very emphatic, I don't know why, but I don't see..."

"Oh my God!" Anna cried. "Oh Malcolm, you fool. You bloody, bloody fool!"

"What, Anna, what is it?" Simon said turning towards her, a look of alarm on his face.

"Jodie was pregnant," Anna wailed. "She confided in me just after I got here. That's why she and Martin weren't getting on this afternoon. She was determined to have the child, but he wanted nothing to do with it. He'd said he wanted her to have an abortion."

"I'm not sure I quite understand," Simon said, "what exactly are you saying, Anna?"

"Oh I see," Malcolm said slowly, sitting down on the edge of the coffee table and holding his head in his hands. "If she was pregnant, then in effect there were two of them. The elixir was shared and... and I have just made a terrible mistake."

There was silence in the room for a moment. Then the doorbell rang.

The three friends turned and looked as one towards the hallway, unable to move or speak, their faces frozen in the dreadful realisation of the moment.

The doorbell rang again.

NEVER FORGET A FACE

It's a strange thing, but I have lived in London for most of my life, yet I've never walked down Harley Street before. It's a household name, isn't it? Up there in lights with the likes of Portobello Road and Carnaby Street. But for some reason it just doesn't seem to be one of those places you stumble upon by accident, while you're busy trying to get somewhere else. Odd, really, when you consider that it's so central, a mere stone's throw from Regents Park tube station.

I came by tube today actually. I certainly wasn't going to risk a taxi. I've had a few bad experiences recently with taxi drivers not turning out to be what they seemed. Best to get lost in the Underground crowds, keeping your head down, avoiding getting noticed. No doubt about this place when you get there, though: Harley Street W1, City of Westminster, clearly displayed on the end wall. You can probably buy replicas of that sign at souvenir shops, along with the ones of Downing Street and Mind the Gap.

Mind you, the actual street itself was a bit of a disappointment for me; I'd expected imposing old buildings with a bit of gravitas, not these monotonous Regency terraces with their mock façades and pretentious porticos. And not a Rolls Royce in sight. It had occurred to me there might be a problem if there were rows of chauffeurs waiting for me outside, but it's all double yellows or "set down only" these days, thank goodness.

Took me a while to find the right door, though. They all look the same from the pavement, from the wrong side of the railings, so to speak. You can't read the names on the brass plates from that distance, you see, especially the ones that haven't been polished properly.

Anyway, here we are then, ready to see the specialist at last and I haven't spotted a single one of *them* on the way here. The clinic reception area is a bit dingy, I think, basically just a cramped hallway full of chintzy soft furnishing. More like a down-at-heel country house hotel than a clinic. But there again, the place is empty apart from the receptionist and she's definitely female, so no worries on that score. Actually, since it's free, I think I'll have some instant in one of those flowery porcelain cups set out on the fancy little table over there. Then I'll just sit and get my thoughts together ready for the specialist. No point in coming all this way to give a rambling, unconvincing account of the problem. Facts are what he is going to want; hard, well ordered facts.

Hard to say exactly when I first noticed something was wrong. A few weeks back now, I guess, when the business about faces started. I kept seeing the same face, you see, popping up everywhere: in the street, at the shops, on the train, you name it. Always complete strangers at first, just passers-by, never saying anything. They didn't even make eye contact back then. And the funny thing was, although they all appeared to be different people, each time you just knew that the face was familiar. In the early days, I was often caught unawares, so they had passed by and gone before recognition dawned.

It got me thinking about faces: I remember trying to work out how human beings manage to identify each other at all. Of course, it isn't just about faces, it's much more subtle than that, isn't it? You can recognise someone by the way they sit or walk, by a gesture of the hand, even just the set of their shoulders or the angle of their head. But the face is the clincher. Always assuming what you might term cultural alignment, that is. Well, the Chinese and Eskimos all look alike to us, but it's not like that amongst themselves, of course. And have you ever tried recognising a face, or even what kind of expression it has, from an upside-down picture? Not possible, I can assure you.

But I'm getting carried away here. The specialist won't want to hear all that, just what's been happening to me. Stay objective, stick to the facts.

Right, well I suppose what I thought at first, back then, was that I was being watched, followed around. It was always a man, never a woman. Funny that. I remember thinking early on that someone might have hired a private detective to spy on me, although I couldn't think for the life of me why anyone would want to do such a thing. Then after a bit, things took a turn for the worse. Complete strangers I had never met before started to greet me, accosting me in the street or the gymnasium changing rooms, wherever: all sorts of places. They would never use my name, but they always gave the impression that they knew me. And the unsettling thing was that their faces were always strangely familiar and always the same. There was something about the way they smiled that I learned to dread. Christ, that smile! There are ordinary smiles, you know, ones that convey happiness, friendship and all that, but there is also a certain kind of smiling face that puts the fear of God into you. The sort of smile that you might expect on the face of a vindictive torturer about to give the rack another turn. And the smile I kept getting confronted with somehow managed to convey a sort of grinning malevolence, just like that.

As time went on, it became more and more apparent to me that I wasn't just being watched, but played with, as a cat does with a mouse. Worse still, I started to suspect that it wasn't just a single person doing this, but a whole legion of watchers, all with the same faces and the same terrible, knowing smile. Of course, I had no idea what they were after – still haven't, even now – and for a while I started to doubt my own sanity over the matter. But just as I had nearly convinced myself that I was imagining it all, another one would pop up: on a bus, in the office, anywhere in fact, and the feeling of menace would return.

After a bit, it became plain to me that I had to take some action, try to avoid them, give them the slip, so as to speak. I started to shun the kinds of places where it seemed they were most likely to catch up with me: small, empty shops, public conveniences, deserted streets, that sort of thing. And taxis. Especially taxis. You can never really tell from the back of a taxi driver's head what he looks like until he turns round to take the fare, and by then you're trapped and it's too late. If I had to go out at all, I figured that crowded public places were the best. Safety in numbers. I quickly learned not to make eye contact with anyone, ever. But *they* were smart, you see, always knowing what I was at, always one step ahead, pitching up with that ghastly smile around every corner. I could swear that there were more and more of them as time went on. They would keep finding me through sheer weight of numbers. Not just as passing strangers in the street, in a sort of random contact strategy, if you will, but as bank clerks, postmen, bus drivers. Even police officers on the beat.

Things really started to come to a head when they moved in next door. I'd never really taken much notice of the neighbours before, but one day I saw the curtains twitch as I was coming home and there was no doubt about it. Even from behind the netting, it was unmistakable: that face, that terrible mocking smile.

Well, obviously, I thought I'd just stop going out at all. It was going to be the only way to defeat them. I remember thinking that I would have to stock up with supplies to last out my siege, so one terrible afternoon I bit the bullet, blitzed the local supermarket, staggered back to the flat loaded with carrier bags and finally closed the door behind me. With a sense of relief, I can tell you.

From then on, I wasn't even going to answer the doorbell. They'd have thought of trying that, you could be sure. But as I'm going to tell the specialist in just a moment, even that didn't work. The very same evening they rumbled me and got inside. I made the mistake of turning on the television for the late night news. The awful moment when the newscaster looked up and smiled out of the screen is burned on my memory. I instantly smashed the set, of course, but it was too late.

That was when I realised I needed to seek professional help. I had to consult someone who would understand and be able to explain what was happening to me. So here I am, sitting in a Harley Street waiting room, thoughts all in order, story ready to tell.

"The doctor will see you now."

★ ★ ★

Well, that was a bit of a disaster, but at least I got home safely. Now I've got all the doors and windows bolted, I think I could do with a stiff drink, at least a couple of fingers. Steady my nerves a bit.

Christ, what an afternoon.

You know, for a while, I really thought I'd done the right thing going there. In with a chance of getting to the bottom of things. The specialist was most reassuring, seemed to know his stuff and everything. Before I went in, I confess I was a bit worried that he might not take me seriously, but it was quite the reverse, I assure you. He seemed fascinated by my account, taking notes, asking intelligent questions every now and again. Then he gave me a good going over. A proper examination: sensation, muscle power, reflexes, the works. Very reassuring he was, too, and careful to emphasise that I was not going mad or anything like that. Apparently my story is classic and I have a well recognised neurological condition. I've got it written down here on a sheet of his notepaper: prosopagnosia.

The way he explained it, you stop being able distinguish faces properly, so other people all start to look the same. And if it happens quite suddenly, the doctors think it's usually due to a small stroke and it often just gets better again on its own after a year or two. All very nice. Then he ruined it a bit by saying he thought I actually had a rather rare "upside down" version of the condition, so the sufferer still recognises other people's faces, but identifies them incorrectly. Often with threatening effect, he said. He wrote the name of this other condition down for me, too. Here we are. The Capgras Delusion, that's what he called it. Well, at first I just thought that didn't sound quite so good, but at least I've still got a proper diagnosis. Then something made me look up at him carefully again and I realised there was a serious problem with all this.

The specialist was smiling at me. And suddenly I realised: he was one of them.

SKY BURIAL

For a moment, Matthew thought the imposing boulder which loomed ahead through the mist was familiar; one of the landmarks that had caught his attention on the climb up. But no, another disappointment. The weirdly-sculpted granite formations on this mountainside all looked very similar, especially in poor weather conditions. He was thoroughly lost and he knew it.

The mountain peak had appeared an easy objective from the little village square below where he had spent so much time these last few days, sitting outside the café, drinking espresso and sometimes pastis. And so it had proved, to begin with, as he had set off this morning with the promise of yet another fine day before him. The steep, rough alleys at the upper edge of the village had quickly led him to a myriad of goat tracks, through prickly scrub and then out onto the rocky slopes of the mountainside. There had been no proper path leading up towards the summit, but an obvious route presented itself, first weaving through the giant boulders and then diagonally up the crest of a rocky ridge. Indeed, once he had reached the top an easy hour of walking later, his entire route of ascent and the distant village below had been plainly visible.

There had also been a marvellous panorama of the surrounding countryside, making the effort of the climb seem more than worthwhile. It had been a wonderful moment. But then the mist had come rolling in from the north side of the mountain, lapping up the slopes with unexpected speed and shrouding everything in a dense, damp greyness. At first Matthew had been sure that he could simply retrace his steps and make his way safely down despite the poor visibility, but without definite landmarks he had become increasingly disorientated by the shrouded, rocky landscape

Turning from the huge boulder, he decided to climb back upwards, in the hope of identifying the base of the steep ridge which he had followed on the last part of his climb to the summit.

Then, as he picked his way over the uneven ground, there was a sudden sound of rushing air just above his head. He looked up to see a large, dark object sweeping across his path and back into the mist. The silence quickly closed around him again. For a moment his heart pounded in panic, but then he remembered the fine pair of Egyptian vultures he had seen circling high above him back at the summit, lazily soaring without a single beat of their huge wings. The dense mist must have curtailed their hunt for carrion and driven them down close to ground level.

He climbed on, but a few moments later he was

brought to a startled halt by a towering black shadow which suddenly loomed up in front of him. It was a sheer rock escarpment, and there was no way round it. Now he knew he was on alien territory. He had clearly strayed further than he first thought. There no longer seemed any hope that he would be able to find a recognisable part of his outward route.

Suddenly tired, he stopped to rest on a boulder beneath the cliff face and began to wonder how long it would be before anyone missed him and raised the alarm. Not before nightfall, he thought. The village was tiny, a typical Mediterranean hill settlement with more sheep and goats in its narrow dirt streets than there were human inhabitants, and no other foreigners except himself. The landlady of the taverna at which he was staying, the only one in the village, was unlikely to become concerned until well after dark, when the evening meal was normally served.

As he sat considering his predicament, he became aware of a throbbing discomfort in the back of his head. This pain he knew well; it was what had driven him to seek medical help six months ago back in England. Following the initial consultation and tests, the transition from health and freedom to despair had been swift. A tumour of the brain, he had been told. They would operate at once to take samples in order to find out what kind of growth it was.

He remembered starkly the morning in the surgical ward when one of the doctors had come to tell him the bad news. Malignant and inoperable. Nothing could be done. The surgeon had taken as much of the tumour away as possible, in order to try and relieve the symptoms in the short term, but they had told him it would inevitably grow back in a very few months. He had refused the offer of radiation treatment, at best palliative and certain to produce unpleasant side effects, and had determined to leave the grey English winter skies behind while he still could. Matthew had no particular ties or close family at home and the idea of trying to recover some of his strength in a sunnier and more peaceful environment had seemed the most attractive option open to him.

It had, of course, occurred to him that he might never see England again, but that in itself had made the plan seem preferable to any alternative. He had a morbid dislike, almost a phobia, of hospitals, and his instincts had persuaded him that it would be better to die in freedom and anonymity. It had been unfortunate that the coastal resort he had picked from the travel agent's brochure had turned out to be so noisy and busy, despite its outwardly charming appearance. In the end, the sheer number of tourists jostling for place in the streets had driven him to make enquiries about possible places to stay in the hills behind the town. Forbidden to drive after the surgery, he had finished up on a local bus, laboriously winding up the steep, narrow mountain roads above the resort, crammed in alongside elderly black-clad women, cackling fowl and crates of vegetables.

A scratching noise disturbed his troubled thoughts. He looked up to see one of the giant birds perched on a boulder not twenty metres above him, its hooked outline unmistakable even through the mist. Moments later, the second one appeared out of the gloom, swooping low on broad outstretched wings to perch alongside its mate, briefly extending its long neck as it did so. In other circumstances it would have been a privileged moment, but as things stood the appearance of these rather sinister scavengers, especially in the grey, misty silence, only served to increase his sense of unease.

The throbbing pain in Matthew's head was becoming quite unpleasant. They had warned him that it would return and that he should seek medical help again immediately if it did. Not really an option at the moment, even if he had wanted to, he thought grimly.

An overwhelming sense of fatigue now came over him. He was going to have to rest before continuing. He made himself as comfortable as possible, sat with his back against one of the rocks and closed his eyes for a few moments. Despite the pulsing headache, he was feeling more than a little drowsy. Gradually a blessed oblivion overcame him.

★ ★ ★

He was descending quite rapidly now, the steep and uneven rocky terrain giving way to easier, more level ground. A faint track became apparent underfoot and the air lightened, promising an end to the dense mist at last. It was definitely not the way he had climbed up from the village, but that did not matter. He could easily seek help and directions when he came to the first place of habitation.

As the mist gradually parted, he continued downwards with an increasing lightness of heart. The grass and flowering scrub gave off a pleasant scent after that of the damp rocks higher up and slowly but surely the sun started to break through the mist, warming his chilled bones. The view that began to materialise below was an attractive one: a lush hanging valley, bounded by woodland and more distant mountains, with a gurgling stream at his feet which swelled into a broad river further down.

He stopped to scoop up some water from the brook and to survey the scene. There was a certain fairytale quality to it. A small, rustic village nestled in the valley bottom and rising up behind it was an impressive stone castle, perfectly preserved and apparently untouched by the numerous wars which he knew had torn this country apart in previous centuries. He felt no anxiety whatsoever at the strangeness of his surroundings, more a feeling of excitement and a sense of adventure. He would walk on down to the village shortly and perhaps seek accommodation for the night there. But first he thought he would rest awhile up here, since it was still broad daylight and there was no rush now. Although his throbbing headache had gone, he still felt very tired and it would do no harm to lie down on the warm grass for a few minutes and soak up the welcome sunshine.

As he settled himself down on the ground, a group of large and elegant white horses emerged from the woods just below and he watched them crossing the meadow to drink from the stream. It did not bother him at all that each of these splendid creatures had a long, pointed horn projecting from the centre of its forehead. He closed his eyes, and this time the sleep was sweet.

* * *

The huge flock of sheep and goats swarmed over the scrubby landscape, on their way back up to summer pastures. But there was something wrong, the goatherd sensed. Two of his dogs, usually diligent workers, had been distracted for some reason and were climbing higher up the mountainside. Whatever they were barking at was just out of sight, in front of a prominent rock escarpment but hidden behind some boulders. Perhaps he should climb up to investigate; the other dogs could be trusted with the flock.

When he reached the rocks, the two dogs stopped barking and withdrew slightly. They had found some bones; big ones, and judging by the skull, human. But they had been picked clean by scavengers and were already becoming bleached by the fierce late spring sun.

A vague memory came into the goatherd's mind of the English tourist who had disappeared from his sister's village two valleys distant last summer. The news of the search and its failure and final abandonment had been the local gossip for a while. Perhaps this was him, the goatherd thought, or perhaps not. But in any case, identification would now be well nigh impossible; nature had done her work too well.

He stood staring at the remains for a few minutes longer, then lightly crossed himself. No point in disturbing things now, best let the poor fellow be. He turned back down the mountainside to rejoin his flock, the two dogs eagerly slipping over the rough ground before him, their distraction forgotten.

None of them noticed that they were being watched. If the goatherd had looked upwards, he would have recognised the hunched, silent outlines of a pair of Egyptian vultures, just breaking the skyline of the cliff which reared up behind them. To the untrained eye, they could almost have been oddly-shaped rocks.

CLOSE TO THE EDGE

The mist was very dense, reducing visibility to only a few feet and completely obscuring the drop into the ravine below. The girl leaned over the low stone wall and wondered why she felt cheated, rather than encouraged, by this obscuration. But it was time to make a move, because the alarm would surely have been raised by now and they would be out looking for her. She knew there would be some urgency in their search because two of the others had given the warders the slip in recent weeks and had not returned. Nothing had been said officially, of course, but word had got about and everyone knew that they had both been hangers. Not something that she could contemplate, even if there was access to a rope: it would take some skill to bring off and so many things could go wrong. But it meant that security had already been tightened and if she were to be taken back it was unlikely she would get a second chance.

"I take it you're considering jumping?"

The voice was a man's, deep and resonant, coming from close by. Startled, she peered into the mist. She could just make out a dark, indistinct figure standing a short distance to one side, next to the parapet.

"Get away, don't come near me or I'll do it, all right?" she shouted, startled. She moved back slightly.

"My dear, I have no intention of trying to stop you, have no fear of that," the figure said, not moving.

"I know what you want, I know your type, you're from the Samaritans. You want to talk me out of it, but I'm not going to let you, just stay away!"

"As a matter of fact, I don't approve of that organisation."

"Why are you here, then, what do you want?"

"Just curious, that's all."

"Well mind your own business! What are you curious about, anyway?

"About you. I don't yet know your name, for example."

"I know your tricks, asking names, trying to get my confidence. I'm not that stupid. Anyway what's yours, Mr Curious?"

"Oh, I'm called by many names, but that's not important to you."

"Well in that case, I'm not telling you mine."

"Touché, my dear, you have a point."

There was a silence. She leaned sideways to try to get a better look at him, but the mist was too dense and she dared not move any closer.

"I suppose," the man said after a few minutes, "that you have thought all this through? I mean that by taking your own life you would be committing mortal sin and condemning yourself in perpetuity?"

"If you mean heaven and hell and all that, forget it, 'cos I don't believe in that kind of thing."

"Oh, I do agree, they are most nebulous and unsatisfactory concepts." He paused for a moment. "But just because you don't believe in something doesn't mean it doesn't exist. Only a child closes its eyes and pretends that not being able to see something will make it cease to exist. I sense you are anything but childish."

"Oh, I get it, so next you'll be telling me that if I jump I'll be roasting in hellfire for ever, or some such nonsense."

"Dear me, not at all. As a matter of fact, have you thought that heaven, if it exists that is, might be rather dull? A sort of, ah - afterlife sentence of boredom, to be avoided at all costs. The other place might even be quite exciting. You shouldn't believe everything people tell you, you know."

"Well I don't believe you either, it's all nonsense. And if I want to end things, there's nothing you can do to stop me." As she spoke, she scrambled up and stood on the top of the parapet. "See? Now bugger off and let me be."

"I can see that you are a very determined young lady" the voice said with a rather irritating chuckle, throaty and self-indulgent. "But one thing still puzzles me. Have you really considered what will happen at the very moment when you land at the bottom of this ravine? Tell me that, at least."

"I'll die, of course. Everything will just end."

"Oh dear, I've heard this sort of thing so often from the misinformed confronting death. You'll be expecting oblivion then, I take it?"

"So often? What do you mean, so often? What are you, some sort of a ghoul who enjoys going round interfering with other people's deaths? Maybe you should get a proper job as an undertaker, you'd get on well with that by the sound of it."

"Oh I'm flattered!" the man chuckled out loud again. "Actually, I suppose I am an undertaker, in one sense, although not the one you're thinking of, I fear. But to return to what we were just talking about, has it occurred to you that landing on the sharp rocks down there might bring you a moment of terrible injury and pain?"

"But I'm going to die instantly, aren't I? So there won't be time to feel pain, clever dick."

"Ah. Instantly. I suppose that might be true from the point of view of a worldly observer, I grant you. But what if that instant is perceived by yourself as one which is never ending, holding you forever in the moment and condemning you to an eternity of pain? Have you thought of that? Perhaps, if it is oblivion you seek, you should seriously consider dying happily amongst all the pleasures that life has to offer. You don't have to let them take you back to the Institute, you know, there's plenty to enjoy out there in the big wide world while you're waiting for a - how shall I put it - a more comfortable death to turn up, in the natural course of things."

"That's bullshit. Haven't found much comfort in my life. Anyway, how do you know about the Institute, I never said nothing about that?"

"I know so many things, my dear, it's part of my job, you see."

"You're just a nosy parker trying to talk me out of jumping, aren't you? Why the fuck can't you just go away? I'm fed up with you trying to confuse me with your fancy words. I told you, if I want to jump down there, I will."

At that moment, as she looked down from the parapet, the mist cleared slightly above them, letting through a hazy sunlight.

"Christ, what the hell's that down there?" she screamed.

With a deft movement, the indistinct figure leaped up onto the parapet, still keeping its distance in the swirling mist.

"Christ and hell together, this I must see!" the voice cried with a sound of glee. "Aha! My poor girl. You've just been frightened by a simple Brockenspectre, how delightful!"

"Don't you make fun of me! Anyway, what's one of those when it's at home, since you're so clever?"

"Just the light projecting your own shadow onto the mist down below. Simple physics, that's all, nothing to do with either heaven or hell, I'm afraid."

"But if that's my shadow...then where..."

"Where is *my* Brockenspectre? Oh bother, I was

hoping you wouldn't notice that. Do you know, I think this mist really is starting to clear. It's been lovely talking my dear, but I'm afraid I really must be off now. Goodbye."

Without warning, the indistinct figure alongside her launched itself off the parapet and into the misty void. She looked on in horror as its dark outline hung suspended for a second, then seemed to spread out sideways before finally disappearing with a single, lazy, wing-like movement. Almost at once the mist finally swirled clear, revealing the immense drop into the ravine below, but no sign of bird or man.

A cold finger of fear went through her with a violent shiver. Then something soft brushed against her leg, making her jump back in alarm and almost lose her balance. Looking down, she saw that it was a large black cat. It arched its back in a threatening fashion. She kicked out at it violently and it screeched, jumped back down off the wall onto the ground and stared back up at her malevolently.

For a brief moment she pondered on the treachery which seeks to ensnare both the living and the dead. Then she turned and leapt into the abyss.

WINTER CONCERTO

I saw Leslie yesterday. Actually, I heard rather than saw him, at first. The music was coming from the narrow alleyway between W H Smiths and Burtons, a place often frequented by buskers. A solo violin was playing the slow movement of the Winter concerto from Vivaldi's *Four Seasons*. It was clearly audible, even above the clamour of a busy Saturday afternoon in a pedestrian shopping mall.

Although it was nearly twenty years since we had last seen each other, I knew at once that the violinist had to be Leslie. Surely no one else could be playing the instrument in quite the same way, with the same quaint affectations of style. And I had good cause to know the particular piece being played as well as I knew the artist. Pausing amongst the jostling crowd of Christmas shoppers, I was transported back to the long, hot summer of my last year at school. The time when I had struggled to master that Vivaldi concerto for myself.

As a young boy, I never really wanted to play the violin. But my father insisted that I take it up, enrolling me for staid and uninspiring group lessons at my school. Unable to play himself, my father was a keen music lover and often took me to concerts, anxious to infect me with his own enthusiasm for the classical repertoire. In particular, I remember the outdoor summer concerts given by the city's Sinfonietta. Every fine Sunday during the season, my father would take me to the park and we would sit in deckchairs ranged around the bandstand, listening to the concert programme, soaking up the sunshine.

It was there that I first saw Leslie, who was then the orchestra's flamboyant concert master and principal soloist. After the scattered applause for the overture had died down, he would step out to the front of the bandstand and give an exaggerated bow to the audience. Then he would turn to start the orchestral *tutti* of the afternoon's concerto, conducting at first with his violin bow. During the solo passages, his tall, gaunt figure would bend and swoop about the stage as he played, punctuating the music with frequent theatrical flourishes. As a boy I was spellbound, seized by the sheer romance of such a spectacle. I suppose it was then that I first made up my mind to take the violin seriously, to try to emulate the amazing sounds that this extraordinary figure could draw out of his instrument.

The second thing that inspired me to persevere with violin playing also led to a remarkable coincidence. For reasons I do not understand, even now, my school's head of music selected me as a candidate for one of the Rural Music School's exhibitions. These gave successful applicants a place in the County Youth Orchestra and, crucially for those from poorer backgrounds, provided a grant to finance private instrumental lessons. I remember little about the audition, though I cannot imagine that my poorly-tutored playing was particularly impressive. However, much to my father's delight, a letter arrived a few days later informing my parents that I had indeed been awarded one of the coveted exhibitions.

I would have to say that I was not at all happy in the youth orchestra at first, sitting at the back of the second violins, getting lost most of the time. It took quite a while to gain sufficient experience and confidence to enjoy orchestral playing. The private violin lessons, in contrast, rapidly became the highlight of my week. It turned out that my teacher was to be none other than the concert master of the Sinfonietta, the same virtuosic figure that had so held me in awe at the promenade concerts.

I remember the very first lesson with Leslie vividly. I had walked straight from school to his apartment, clutching my violin in one hand and a battered old leather music case in the other. I was trembling with nerves by the time I pushed the doorbell, bitterly regretting the exhibition and all that it had brought. But it did not take long for Leslie to put me at ease. Despite his commanding appearance on stage, he had a kindly, reassuring personality and a delightful eccentricity of manner that quickly cured my pubescent shyness. We would begin every lesson with a cup of tea – Earl Grey in huge breakfast cups – and chocolate digestive biscuits. While I consumed them, Leslie would regale me with anecdotes about the professional world of music, never hesitating to gossip scurrilously about the shortcomings of his fellow performers. I felt most privileged and very grown up.

"And the principal oboist of the New Philharmonia is an absolute disaster. I can't think how he got there in the first place. Oh, he's no doubt technically competent, but his playing has no soul, dear boy, absolutely no soul."

When it came to playing music, Leslie was very keen on what he called soul. And to be fair, he did improve my tone within a very few sessions. Even my father noticed when I was practising at home. For Leslie, accuracy of notes was certainly not the most important thing.

"I never mind a few wrong notes, dear boy, nobody does. But you must always play with soul."

In the same vein, he had no patience with those who complained about their instruments. "It's not what you play, dear boy, it's how you play it", he would say.

Indeed, sometimes when I was struggling to get a decent sound from my violin, he would seize it from my hands and proceed to play the music back to me, meaningfully drawing an extraordinary richness and depth of tone, even from such a mediocre instrument.

From the outset I was treated like an adult and made to feel that I really could play. Sometimes, Leslie's particular version of wisdom was positively inspired. Once, for example, when I complained that my left-hand little finger wasn't strong enough to reach for a note, he brought me up with a start.

"We're not athletes! You don't see violinists with bulging finger muscles do you? Playing isn't in the fingers - it's in the mind, dear boy, all in the mind!"

At other times, his eccentricities proved too much for me. I remember attempting some unaccompanied Bach, with rather limited success, when he gently touched my shoulder to stop me, paused, then said gravely:

"You know, dear boy, I sometimes think that Bach is God."

This was followed by a slightly embarrassed silence while he held my gaze, and I vainly searched for a sensible response. Strangely enough, thinking back on that particular pronouncement, I'm not sure he didn't have a point.

Overall, however, Leslie's unconventional but inspired approach to teaching really did pay off. Within months my technique was transformed, as he coaxed me through an increasingly complex repertoire. The dull studies and student pieces from school were left behind as I learned to play real music. Before long, I was starting to tackle the solo parts of some of the easier classical violin concertos. Even the rehearsals of the County Youth Orchestra started to become enjoyable as I gradually worked my way up to the second desk of first violins.

During my weekly lessons with Leslie, he would

stride around the room, gesticulating and commenting as I played. Sometimes he would let me continue, whooping encouragement as I launched into particularly difficult passages.

"Keep going, dear boy, keep going! You're doing splendidly! Remember, it's all in the mind!"

At other times, he would bring me to a halt by throwing his arms into the air and howling in mock anguish.

"No! No! This is torture! If nothing else, you must play it with soul!"

I would then be mortified until, silently and with a sweeping motion of his long arms, he encouraged me to try again. But best of all for me were the lessons when he picked up his own instrument and played duets with me. As I struggled alongside him, the flamboyance and authority of Leslie's playing somehow enabled me to relax and perform better than I could ever have done without him.

As I entered the sixth form at school, weighed down by the anxiety of exams, I remember some particularly golden moments with the Bach Double concerto.

"I think, dear boy," Leslie would announce over the tea cups, "you are looking a little stressed. Shall we do the Bach Double today?"

And throwing all prepared plans for the lesson to the winds, we would wend our way indulgently together through the slow movement of that wonderful piece, Leslie's rich and spacious rendering encouraging me and drawing me forwards on the second line.

It was in my last year at school that things started to come apart. Shortly after Christmas, The Arts Council announced that it was withdrawing its grant for the Sinfonietta as part of a cost-cutting exercise. After a brief struggle to find alternative sources of funding, the orchestra was disbanded and by Easter, Leslie was concert master no longer. He was desolate. I remember one lesson which was almost entirely taken up by Leslie pacing around his apartment, ranting at the state of arts funding in the country and hurling insults at the Arts Council in particular.

"It's a complete disaster, dear boy. They should have axed the New Philarmonia, not us. The people on the Council are philistines! Philistines!"

He was eventually reduced to taking peripatetic teaching jobs in local schools, something that he clearly felt was beneath his dignity. And in the ensuing months I became aware that Leslie was short of money. There were tell-tale signs. The replacement of chocolate digestives by rich tea biscuits, for example. Worse still, I noticed one week that he was no longer using his fine ivory-mounted Tubbs bow. I said nothing, out of politeness, but he knew I had noticed.

"It's a tragedy, dear boy, like losing an old friend. But needs must, you know."

He never actually asked me for money, perhaps sensing (correctly) that I would be both embarrassed and unable to help. God knows, my parents had little enough of their own. But I heard from several sources that he had been asking other people for what he called loans, promising to pay them back but never doing so. It was sad for me to see and hear these things, but I had much to distract me that last year at school. I was studying for three science A-levels and surprised everyone, including myself, by being offered a place at Imperial College to read aeronautical engineering if my grades were good enough. Leslie had tried to get me to apply to the Guildhall to study violin, but my father would not hear of it, despite his own love of music. Under the circumstances, I did not need much persuading that a career as a professional violinist would be just too insecure.

"A loss to the fraternity, dear boy. Who knows what could have been achieved. Your talent will be wasted, quite wasted."

My lessons with Leslie continued through to the end of the summer term, nevertheless. As exams loomed, I found practising the violin a great release from academic study. Despite the slightly strained atmosphere, Leslie continued to encourage me to push my playing to the limits, suggesting an ever more demanding repertoire. During the summer term, he had me tackling the solo violin parts of Vivaldi's *Four Seasons* concertos, pieces I had often heard him perform in his days with the Sinfonietta. There was no doubt that they suited his own flamboyant playing style, and I think we both felt that this project would somehow act as a fitting swansong to my musical apprenticeship. Once exams were over, I remember working very hard to overcome the technical problems involved in their performance. We had started with Spring and then worked through the other three seasons in calendar order. Towards the end of term, I was wrestling with Winter, which I found the hardest and most elusive of the four works.

Then came the ultimate disappointment. For my very last lesson with Leslie, I was to show him what I had made of the Winter concerto. After that, he had promised me one last time playing the Bach Double together. Perhaps because of what happened, I can recall the events of that day vividly. School had effectively finished for the post-exam sixth formers, so the lesson was to be in the early afternoon for a change.

Taking advantage of the glorious weather, I made my way to Leslie's apartment by bicycle, my violin slung over my back. I remember how much I was looking forward to this final tryst with my musical mentor. But he was not there. I waited outside his front door for an age, ringing the bell several times with increasing concern. Eventually I had to give up, returning home puzzled and rather downcast. For all his eccentricities, Leslie had always been totally reliable about giving lessons and nothing like this had ever happened before. I telephoned his number after I got home, but there was no reply.

The truth about Leslie's disappearance came out piecemeal over the ensuing days, mostly in the local newspaper, but later also on the regional television news. A young girl at one of the schools where Leslie taught had apparently complained to her parents about being fondled inappropriately during a violin lesson. Leslie had been arrested on the morning of my planned last lesson and held in police custody. A search of his apartment was said to have revealed compromising photographs. Further allegations quickly followed from other young female pupils, previously too frightened to speak out. In the end, months later, I heard that Leslie had been convicted of several paedophile offences and given a seven-year custodial sentence.

Initially, I was gutted. I felt somehow dirty myself, sullied by my long relationship with Leslie and betrayed by what he had done. Over the years I had come to respect him not just as a musician and teacher, but also as a person; a role model, if you will. For a while I became angry, not so much with Leslie himself as with the appalling sordidness which had so suddenly entered my pristine world of youth, hope and opportunity. The spell had been well and truly broken.

Fortunately, other events took over. Very soon afterwards, my exam results came through and to my delight I found that I had achieved top grades. Within days, Imperial College confirmed my place for the coming term and I was quickly plunged into preparations for going up to London to start a new life as an undergraduate engineering student. Knowing that I had to try to put the past behind me, it was nonetheless with very mixed feelings that I eventually resolved to leave my violin at home. I had not touched the instrument since the fateful day of my last lesson and I found that the association with Leslie was just too painful. In the end, I never played the violin again. My father was upset at the time, of course, and very embarrassed about the whole affair. We did not discuss it much, but in time I think he accepted my decision. My mother refused to even mention the matter.

So the last music I played on the violin was the Winter concerto. The very same music that now echoed through the shopping mall on an appropriately cold and wintry December Saturday.

"Excuse me, mate, but are you all right? You look as though you've just seen a ghost."

The man stood peering at me over an armful of parcels, then, seeming to realise that I did not want his attention, moved off into the throng of other Christmas shoppers. I realised that I had been standing in a trance for some minutes, oblivious to the heaving crowds around me.

The violin had moved onto the last movement of the concerto, its sound now competing with that of carol singing coming from further down the precinct. At first, I decided to walk away and continue my own shopping, to turn my back on the affair for a second time. But somehow I found myself moving towards the alleyway, drawn irresistibly to the sound of Vivaldi's most famous work. I turned the corner, leaving the bustling crowds behind.

And there he was. Standing in a disused shop doorway, an open violin case containing a few coins at his feet and a frayed blanket draped around his shoulders. Older, gaunt and shabby, but still unmistakeably Leslie. His hands looked blue with the cold, but he was somehow managing to play with much of his old power and vigour ("It's all in the mind, dear boy"), his eyes closed, a rapt expression on his face. I stood for a moment, listening, feeling numb inside. Then the emotions came flooding in: disappointment, shame, anger, a confused muddle of long-dormant feelings. And, yes, amongst these, pity.

But quite suddenly, I realised that I did not want to speak to him again. I did not even want him to see me. The music was rapidly drawing to a close; I had to leave.

Pulling a ten-pound note from my wallet, I silently dropped it into the open violin case. Then I turned and fled back into the safety of the shopping crowds, praying that his eyes had, indeed, been closed.

THE DOLL'S HOUSE

The nightmare returned last night, its vice-like grip torturing my sleep for the first time in many years. Since burning the doll's house, I had thought myself free of the whole ghastly affair, able to sleep undisturbed once again and wake without fear. But now the horrors of that first morning have come flooding back, and I am overcome with a sense of unutterable despair. It is clear that the terror survived purging by fire and still stalks my subconscious mind, lurking in the darkness, biding its time.

There is only one course of action left. If I cannot destroy or suppress the memory, than I must confront it. I am determined. I will set down the events exactly as they occurred, in a connected account. Whatever becomes of me, the truth shall be known and it will survive my fate.

I only hope that whoever finds this document will believe the words I have written.

★ ★ ★

The doll's house had originally belonged to my grandmother, and it had dominated her dark and heavily-furnished living room since my earliest memories as a child. The wooden panels of the front façade had been permanently removed and were propped up against the wall behind. At first, I remember my mother holding me up in her arms so I could see into the lower rooms, but later I was able to climb the steps in front of the wooden stand that supported the house, clinging to the handrail and standing on tiptoe to see into the upper floors.

I suppose that these days dolls' houses are traditionally the playthings of growing girls, but this was no ordinary childhood toy. Standing a good four feet above its supporting base, it was a colossal achievement, a showcase of nineteenth-century workmanship worthy of any serious museum collection. And as a little boy, I was fascinated by it, entranced by the intimate nature of all its rooms. Here was a house redolent of a domestic existence I could only guess at, but so wished I could be part of. Oh, to be small enough to go in myself!

Of course, in those days I could not appreciate the supreme artistry of the miniaturist: original artworks hanging on the walls, exquisitely-decorated bone china tableware, individually-upholstered soft furnishings, finely-chiselled wooden furniture, hand-painted wallpapers. These things I came to appreciate much later, as an adult collector and specialist in the toys and mechanical artefacts of the late nineteenth century.

Back then, with childish eyes, it was the miniature inhabitants of the house and their daily life that seemed most important. On the lower ground floor, a fat cook reigned supreme in front of the range and cooking pans of the kitchen, complete with its dangling plaster hams and the brightly-coloured vegetables on the scrubbed pine table. There were scullery maids there too, all in their starched white aprons and frilly hats.

Service stairs led up to the next storey, where the opulently-furnished living rooms were inhabited by the moustachioed master of the house and his pretty wife in her yellow silk dress. The study was a particular fascination, its walls lined by miniature leather-bound books, each of which could be removed and opened to reveal hand-written quotations from literature.

A grand central staircase, complete with a balustrade in polished wood, a hand-woven Turkish runner and an ornate glass chandelier, led up to the third floor. The lavishly-appointed master bedroom was on the left side of the landing, its dressing table bearing perfect, tiny replicas of silver brushes and scent bottles, whilst the children's rooms were on the right, including the schoolroom with its miniature blackboard, maps and globe. I should mention that the inhabitants of all the rooms had stayed in exactly the same places (and, indeed, in the same poses) for as long as I could remember, although they were intricately jointed and could have been freely moved at will.

I will come to the top floor in a moment.

When my grandmother died, much of her estate was bequeathed to numerous cousins, with whom I had had little contact over the years. But to my delight, her will was quite specific in leaving the doll's house to me. Whether this was because my grandmother knew of my professional interests, or whether she simply remembered my childhood fascination with the piece, I shall never know. Suffice it to say, I was delighted with the news and had it moved into my own house straight away, using a reliable firm which handled delivery and dispatch of the larger items passing through my shop. I recall spending a wet afternoon happily removing the protective packaging from each room in turn, painstakingly repositioning the loose fixtures and displaced items and putting the figures back exactly as I remembered them.

It was only then that I really took much notice of the top floor. Perhaps it had always been a bit too high for me to see into properly as a child, or perhaps I was simply more interested in the adult world downstairs at that age. But on that rainy afternoon, I gave the top floor the same careful and informed scrutiny as the rest of the house, and quickly noticed that several things were wrong. In real life, in houses of this kind from the era of service, the top floor was usually given over to the nursery, a nanny's room, laundry facilities and suchlike. But in this model, I noticed that the contents of the nursery, including the baby in its cot, had been crammed into a small room in the top right corner of the house, a room of a size perhaps more suitable for linen storage and ironing. Meanwhile, to the left of the upper landing, where the nursery and nanny's quarters should have been, there was a single, large, shallow room almost entirely filled by trunks, hatboxes and surplus furnishings, all stacked on top of each other right up to the ceiling. The figure of the nanny, I now realised, had always been placed in the schoolroom downstairs.

I determined that same afternoon to try and rectify things a little. The remainder of the house was so beautifully correct in every period detail that it seemed a shame to leave the top floor as it was. As I said, I could not clearly remember whether things had been like that on my childhood visits to my grandmother, but seen all those years later through adult eyes, I thought it most likely that the rooms at the top of the house had been a victim of an earlier upheaval, perhaps when my grandparents had emigrated from Germany before the war.

In any event, I worked late into the evening that day, rearranging and restoring the top rooms as my experience told me they should be. First, I removed the piled-up contents of the left-hand room, arranging them on a nearby work surface. Amongst the various items of furniture there, I noted an iron-framed bed, a copper bath tub and other items suitable for a wet nurse or nanny's room. Convinced that I was restoring things as they had been originally, I then removed the contents of the small nursery and carefully rebuilt the small room as a proper nanny's room, relocating the figure of the nanny there when the room was ready.

Then I turned my attention to the larger room on the left of the stairwell. With all the bric-à-brac removed, I could see that this room was in a dreadful state of neglect, making a huge contrast with the near-perfection of the remainder of the house. Using period materials and with the utmost patience, I unblocked the crudely walled-off fireplace and rebuilt it, finishing with tiny pieces of coal and flames of red silk. Then I repapered the entire room with pieces of Victorian flock and assembled all the artefacts and furnishings appropriate for a nursery, using spare pieces from my own collection where necessary.

It was when I was nearly finished with this work, hanging curtains at the room's side window, that one more strange thing occurred to me. On the floors below, the larger rooms had two windows in the outer sides of the doll's house, each casement lovingly glazed with pieces of real glass. On the top floor, two windows were again visible on the left side of the house from the outside, but from the inside of my newly restored nursery only one was apparent. It seemed that there must be a further room or space behind, but with no door or visible means of access. Puzzled, I used a torch to try and peer in through the rear window, but the glass panes had been blackened somehow, preventing a view within. I remember thinking that I should investigate this anomaly further at some stage, but by then the hour was late and I was tired from my labours. Tomorrow, perhaps, I thought.

In the small hours of the long night that followed, the nightmare visited me for the first time. Every detail of its terrible sequence is burned on my memory. I tremble to recall them even now.

I seemed to awake from sleep in a strange house, in near total darkness. Stumbling out of the bedroom door, vaguely aware of not having really woken, I found a dimly-lit stairwell. Descending to the floor below, I could see a strip of light coming from under one of the doors leading off the landing and, reaching forward in the gloom, I opened the door. This revealed a softly-lit room, heavily furnished in nineteenth century style. A man and a woman were sitting either side of a bright fire burning in the hearth. As I entered the room, they both turned towards me and smiled, as if they were expecting me. They were not human, but instead had the jerky movements and painted china faces of dolls.

I slammed the door closed again and a terrible fear overtook me. I realised not only that I was still asleep, but that I was somehow inside the doll's house I had laboured over all the previous evening.

Worse was to follow. There then began loud thumps and crashing noises from the top of the house, echoing down the stairwell. These were soon accompanied by agonising screams. The noise was deafening.

As if drawn by some power outside my control, I began to climb the stairs. Passing the first landing, I continued upwards, aware that the steps seemed to be extending ever further beyond me the higher I climbed, unfolding endlessly into the darkness above. As I paused for breath, leaning on the balustrade, the crescendo of bangs and screams from above was interrupted by a deafening crash, then silence.

At that moment, I found myself in a long corridor, dimly lit by a gas lamp at the far end and lined by doors on either side. This no longer matched the doll's house I thought I knew and I was overcome once again by a suffocating fear, an inchoate premonition of absolute terror.

Then the crashing and rhythmic thumping started again. Its source was not visible, but the noise was clearly emanating from around a corner at the far end of the corridor. With every passing second it was not only getting louder, but closer. Panicking, I reached to open one of the side doors, only to feel my fingernails strike smooth plaster: all the doors and their handles were just painted onto the corridor walls. The stairwell I had ascended was nowhere to be seen. There was no escape.

I awoke in darkness, bathed in sweat, groping furiously for the bedside lamp, praying that my awakening was real. My bedroom was reassuring and peacefully quiet, and I realised just how deafeningly loud the nightmare had been. That first time, I did not dare let myself fall asleep again. I read until dawn with the light on.

Now comes the worst part.

It was mid-morning before I went back to the room where I had set up the doll's house the previous day. The scene that greeted me was as unexpected as it was appalling. Everything spoke of a frightening violence. Before retiring the previous night, I had replaced the front elevation covers of the house, admiring the detail of the portico and stonework. The first thing I saw was that these covers had been ripped off and flung across the room, as if in anger. Then I saw, to my horror, that every room in the doll's house had been totally wrecked: fittings torn down, carpets ripped up, artefacts smashed and strewn about. It was as if something terrible had rampaged through the house, floor by floor, room by room, intent on utter destruction. And yet no one had been in my apartment all night other than myself. I had already checked at first light that all my windows and the front door were still locked and bolted.

As for the inhabitants of the doll's house, none were to be found. I searched the area around the wooden stand in vain: they had completely vanished. Inevitably, my attention was then drawn to the rooms on the top floor. Here the evidence of violent destruction was even more abundant; indeed, it rather looked as though a fire had raged in the room I had newly arranged as a nursery, its walls and ceiling blackened. Amid the other debris, the baby and its cradle lay shattered into fragments, the only remains of the figures I ever found.

Finally, to my utter horror, I saw that a large jagged hole had been punched in the rear wall of the room, the wall that I had suspected was false the previous evening. Nothing was visible beyond but darkness.

I burned the doll's house that very morning, without a shadow of regret, lugging it all out into the garden and dousing everything with paraffin. I remember that I was still shaking as I struck the match. I knew then that I should not have tampered with the house, that in so doing I had released something unspeakably abominable. I prayed that the consuming flames would purge it.

At first, the nightmare did not appear banished by this act, nor the crushing fear that came with it. I was revisited several times over the ensuing months, but mercifully with ever-decreasing frequency. Eventually, however, after a whole year free of it, I had dared to hope myself cured, cleansed by fire, of my terrible dream.

Until last night, that is.

FINAL PERFORMANCE

People say that all old theatres are haunted, their stage boards impregnated by the dramas and tensions of countless performances. It surely has to be so. The very fabric of these places, their stones, plaster and upholstery, cannot possibly retain the sparkling innocence of the new construction which greeted their inaugural performances on opening nights. Not after witnessing centuries of powerful theatrical dialogues, orchestral climaxes, rousing choruses, impassioned arias.

The very efforts of the performers themselves add immeasurably to this process; their sweat and toil, the nerves of opening nights, the leaping physical strength of dancers and the hours of painstaking work which have gone into the rehearsals, all these contribute to the enormous, indefinable energy of the stage. And the audience, the massed crowds of humanity coming to be entertained, can only absorb so much of this energy as it rebounds into the auditorium. The rest must be taken up by the building itself, settling into its structure, performance after performance, layer upon layer, like sediment settling over millennia upon the bed of an ocean.

Some of this pent-up energy is bound to leak back out, now and again, when the theatre is dark and empty after the night's performance has finished. So it is not surprising that many stories of theatre haunting have been told over the ages.

But here is one you have not heard before.

* * *

They made an odd couple, the violinist long-limbed, thin and stooping, the double bass player short, brawny and barrel-chested. But although they played on opposite sides of the orchestra, they were often to be found together after a performance, going off in search of a bar which would serve them a drink. The two of them walked now in the fading twilight down the narrow cobbled streets of an old medieval town, hemmed in by a jumble of fantastical wood and stone buildings overhanging each other at crazy angles.

"Not much of an audience tonight," Olef, the short one, said to his friend.

"What can you expect from a backwater rural town like this?" Karl replied, tucking his violin case more securely under his arm. "Our tours should stick to places of artistic excellence, where we are properly appreciated."

"Strange, though," Olef mused. "It was mostly young people there tonight. You'd think it was a predominantly ageing population in such a remote area."

"Well, the older ones are probably just uneducated peasants. They wouldn't even know what ballet was," said Karl haughtily.

"Steady on, Karl, that's a bit nasty even for you."

"Sorry, it's probably just my heartburn talking," the violinist replied. "But you know what I mean. It's hardly worth bringing the Imperial Ballet to this bohemian country at all, let alone this god-forsaken town."

"But you know the Minister of Culture's views on taking artistic excellence out to the masses," Olef said cynically.

"Balls to the Minister of Culture!" Karl growled. "And I don't know about you, but I need a drink."

"Speaking of which," said Olef, "I noticed old Gregor slip out of the pit again tonight, during the long pas de deux. He only just made it back for his entry this time."

"Well, I'd slip out for a quick one if I had 400 bars rest. Except of course, violinists never have rests. If they paid us all according to the number of notes we played, now that would be something!"

"Ah, but it's not the number of notes," Olef replied. "It's their quality. Not to mention the size and weight of the instrument you have to hold up all evening."

"I sometimes imagine," Karl said, "the way you hold it, that you were actually born wrapped around your double bass."

"Which one?" said Olef smiling. "I only ever use my second best one on tour, you know."

"Oh, basses are ten a penny!" replied Karl mischievously. "Now violins, that's different. With the quality of mine, you know, I could never accept to play on second best".

And so it went on, as they strolled down the maze of narrow streets. These were all familiar arguments, and in truth, the two men liked nothing better than to spar with each other. It was their way of unwinding after a performance. That and a drink or two, of course.

"This looks all right, what do you think?"

Olef stopped and pointed to the front of a building which was seemingly even older than its ancient neighbours. It had crooked, overhanging eaves supporting a wooden inn sign depicting three barrels. The door looked forbidding, studded as it was with iron bolts, but a welcoming orange light shone from the thickly-leaded windows either side.

"It'll do as well as anything," Karl said, and pushed open the door.

The inside of the tavern consisted of a single room with low beams and a quiet, smoky atmosphere. Apart from the glow of a log fire in a huge stone hearth, the only light came from two lanterns hanging above the bar. A group of elderly men were gathered around a table near the fire talking in hushed tones, and a large hound lay asleep in the middle of the floor.

Picking their way carefully around the dog, Karl and Olef went up to the bar and rang a small brass bell apparently left there for the purpose. The barman appeared almost at once, wizened and elderly with a long grey moustache. Without a word, he produced two pewter tankards, filled them from the single large wooden barrel standing on a rack behind and set them on the bar. He eyed them carefully, taking in their formal evening dress and the violin case which Karl had leaned against the wall to one side.

"You've been playing at the Godzny, then" he said, more as an observation than a question.

"That's right," Karl said, "but not many of your townsfolk saw fit to come and hear us. You can't get many opportunities for entertainment in a town like this. You'd think there'd be more interest."

"Ah, the theatre is not much now," the old man said, "although I think the local band plays there occasionally." Glancing across at the group sitting in front of the fire, he dropped his voice. "To tell you the truth, the older folk don't like to go near there these days, especially after dark. They've been around long enough to remember the accident."

Karl and Olef leant closer, sensing some pleasing scandal.

"And what accident was that?" said Olef.

"Well, back a while we had a good state ballet company. They came round on tour once a year, regularly. But their coach got involved in a bad smash not far from here, and it killed many of the best dancers, not to mention folk in the orchestra. The Godzny was the last place they'd been performing, just the night before. Well, since then," the barman's voice dropped still further, "they say you can hear the sound of music coming from inside the theatre at night, even though there's no one there. There's not many that will want to talk about it around here these days, but it was a funny business, you can take my word for it."

Karl shot a conspiratorial glance at his friend, took a long swig from his tankard and sniffed loudly.

"You'd be amazed," he said, "how many theatres claim to be haunted. Yet I've never heard or seen any evidence for these stories. And I've been playing in the oldest and most famous buildings around the world for nearly twenty years."

"I hear what you're saying, but believe me, this one is different," the barman said sadly. "I reckon you should be glad to be off tomorrow. Best to be away from this place."

"Well, as a matter of fact we are away tomorrow," Karl replied haughtily. "And I hope we find a more willing and appreciative audience at our next port of call."

He picked up his violin case and turned to leave. Olef looked embarrassed.

"Don't mind him, he doesn't mean any harm" he said quietly, putting money from his pocket onto the bar. "Goodnight." He made his way quickly back around the sleeping hound and hastened after his friend out onto the street.

It was now almost entirely dark and there was no

one else left abroad. The empty streets were rather inadequately lit by old-fashioned bracket lamps, which cast uneven shadows across the cobbles and onto the façades of the nearby buildings.

"Well, what did you make of that?" Olef demanded of his colleague.

"Stuff and nonsense, if you ask me," Karl replied. "Just a cock and bull story, probably because he was embarrassed about the poor turnout for our performance this evening."

"I'm not so sure," Olef said. "And I'm also just a bit curious. What do you say we go past the theatre on our way back to the hotel, just to see if we do hear anything odd? I don't think it's far out of our way."

"Olef, I'm surprised at you, a bassist turned ghost hunter, eh? Well if you're going back that way, I'll come too. Apart from anything else, I don't fancy getting lost down these streets on my own. As a matter of fact I've no idea of the way back to the theatre, have you?"

"It was next to the church with that tall spire you can still just make out above the roofs over there," Olef said, pointing. "Let's head in that direction. Here, I think this is the one we came down."

He plunged into a dark, narrow alley opposite the tavern, closely followed by his friend clutching his violin case. After a few false turns, they emerged into the small square in front of the theatre and stopped to gather breath. A gibbous moon had risen above the rooftops, casting a silvery light over the ornate stone facade which reared above them. A row of windows set into the upper part of the stonework were in darkness and the building appeared lifeless. Once the echoes of their own footsteps had ceased a dense, palpable silence filled the square.

"Well, I can't hear anything, can you?" Karl was whispering, without quite knowing why.

"Not even a mouse," Olef whispered back. "Tell you what, let's see if we can get in through the stage door round the back, I'll bet it's not locked."

Before his friend could protest, he started off down the dark alley to one side of the theatre, Karl once again scurrying after him, not wanting to be left alone. It was pitch dark around the back of the building, but Olef triumphantly produced a small torch from his pocket.

"I never travel anywhere without one," he whispered. "I don't trust the power supply in these backward countries."

By the light of the torch beam, the two men arrived at the stage door they had used earlier in the evening and, without much surprise, found it unlocked. There was a labyrinth of low ceilinged corridors beyond, interrupted every now and again by peeling baize doors and small flights of steps. At length, they emerged into a much larger space, the tiny beam of Olef's torch barely reaching the walls and ceiling.

"This must be the grand circle foyer," Olef whispered. "I remember the bar over there, I came up here for a drink in the interval."

"Well perhaps we can help ourselves to another," Karl said, "if they haven't locked it all away, of course."

Following the torch beam, he moved over behind the bar and began to rattle the doors of the bottle cabinets.

"Hush!" Olef whispered, suddenly turning off his torch. "Listen. Can you hear anything?"

The two men stood very still, their ears straining in the darkness. At first there was nothing but a blanket of silence, but after a few moments there came the faint but unmistakable sound of music, a single plaintive melody line. Olef turned on the torch again and swung it round onto the padded double doors which led through into the auditorium.

"It's coming from through there," he whispered. "It can't be one of our lot, they'd never come back here to practise, especially at this hour. I'm going to take a look."

"Well I'm not staying here on my own in the dark," Karl whispered back, coming up to the doors behind his friend.

Olef gently pushed open one of the doors and they peered through. The cavernous space of the auditorium was not dark as they expected, but dimly lit by a faint bluish light, seeming to be come from somewhere above the elaborate proscenium arch out in front of them. The music was louder now, the sound clearly that of a solitary flute. Together, they moved hesitantly down the steeply raked centre aisle, between rows of empty seats which faded away into the gloom either side. From the front balcony rail, the stalls below them were barely discernible, but the stage was clearly visible in the eerie light. There was no-one to be seen.

"The flautist must be in the pit" Karl whispered, "but it's too dark to see into it from here."

At first, they thought the stage was completely empty, but then something very strange happened.

"Look! What's that?"

Karl followed the line of Olef's finger and saw what appeared to be a small puff of dust rising up from the stage boards, as if someone had dropped something without making any sound. Then another appeared a short distance away and another, each successive disturbance of the dusty surface keeping time with the music. They stared at the scene for several seconds before slowly realising what they were looking at.

The puffs of dust appeared to mark the rhythmic footfalls of a dancer, slowly moving around the dusty stage in a choreographed pattern. But whoever, or whatever, was making these elegantly-placed steps was completely invisible.

The two friends stared in silent horror, not daring to move or speak. Then, before rising fear had time to take a grip, the unseen flautist came to the end of the melody and the ghostly footfalls ceased. There was a moment's complete silence, and then the two men turned without a word and started back up the aisle.

As they did so, a low murmuring or rustling sound began to emanate from the darkened rows of empty seats all around them. Before they had time to think, the noise developed into a deafening crescendo, echoing around the whole auditorium. It was the unmistakable and familiar sound of thunderous applause from a full house. Yet there was not a soul in sight.

As one man, Karl and Olef fled.

They did not speak of their experience, either to each other or any of their colleagues, but as the orchestra's coach left the town the next day, Olef couldn't help thinking again of the tavern keeper's story from the evening before. And as he did so, a horrible thought occurred to him. He turned to his friend sitting in grim silence beside him.

"I do hope," Olef said, "that history will not repeat itself today."

Printed in Great Britain
by Amazon